MW00881607

Jmm Adams
To Lilly Ivy)
Enjoy to
Follow your
dreams
always.
Michele

SOPHIA and the STRADIVARIUS

A Sophia and Kanani Mystery

By J.M.M.Adams

Apple Cove Press

www.jmmadams.com
www.house-barrett.com

Book Cover Artist: Roslyn McFarland

Editor: Richard Perfrement

Titles by J.M.M. ADAMS

Kanani's Golden Caves

Sophia and the Stradivarius

(Appearing in *First String* this year at the Indie Film Festivals in Asia, Europe, World Wide.)

Sophia and the Dragon

The Russian Spy

The Mystery of Sandy Island

The Mystery of St. Moritz

Be sure to check out Michele's other books at

www.jmmadams.com

http://amzn.to/2bhoEeZ

The book is Dedicated to all
Canines in the military, police
dept., and other departments;
keeping us safe from evil.
May God always look over them
with protection
and love.

CONTENTS

Book Preview

Author

1

THE BLUE SKY TURNED DARK and heavy rain pelted down on my windows. I decided to close my antique shop early today, because of the weather.

The bell over my front door chimed and I looked up. A tall woman clutching a violin case stood just inside the frame. Rainwater soaked through her black, cropped–short hair, and ran down her knee-length, white raincoat. She didn't look very happy.

"It's wet out there, isn't it? What can I help you with?" The door had blown open, so I walked in front of the counter, walked past the woman and closed the door.

"I am looking for a woman named Sophia Anderson. I have travelled a long way to deliver this violin to her from her grandfather. He thought Sophia had moved to Port Townsend and opened an antique shop. I have been to several of them and they weren't the right ones. This is my last hope, then I'm going back home. I've had it with Seattle weather."

"My grandfather sent you? You're in luck, I'm Sophia." I stuck out my hand to greet the woman.

"Thank goodness," she said placing the violin case down and shaking my hand. "My name is Rachael McFarland, it's nice to finally meet you."

"Same here; let me see this violin."

"I believe your grandfather put something in here for you." She handed me the violin.

"I did this as a favor for him. He is an old friend of my grandfather and father, they are luthiers and your grandfather is too. That is how they became such good friends many years ago. I don't know anything more. I must really go, I can't stay." She turned and ran out the door. I carefully put the violin down and ran after her.

"Wait, where did you come from?" I called out.

"Luxembourg, I must really go. Nice meeting you," Rachael called back before turning the corner. I couldn't do anything but watch her disappear. Then as I turned to go back into my shop, I had a glimpse of someone following Rachael.

It's just probably someone running for the ferry too. I thought.

I ran back into my shop without getting too soaked and slammed the heavy door shut, locking it. I had to get home, Kanani, my German Shepherd, must have to go out. I usually bring her with me to work, but with the weather so bad I left her home today. I picked up the violin case and took it into my office placing it on my desk. After putting on my raincoat, I grabbed an umbrella and the violin case. I ran out the back door and made a mad dash down the alley to my car.

I had to run through large puddles, muttering to myself, "I wish I had worn boots today." My feet were soaked, and I was drenched.

Why am I living here? I could be back in Hawaii basking in the sun. I finally got to my car and jumped in. Looking at the clock on my dash, it was only five pm. Hawaii was three hours behind, so I decided to wait and call my husband, John, later.

Ring Ring Ring. *My cell phone's ringing. Darn it's stuck in my pocket.* I fished it out just before it stopped ringing.

"Hello."

"Hi, Sophie, it's me Susan. I'm at the market, I thought I could pick up a pizza and we could eat dinner together tonight."

"That's a great idea, I'm wet, hungry and cold. I'm on my way home now, just come over as soon as you can. I have some wine already, so we don't need anymore. I can't wait to tell you about my strange encounter a little while ago in the shop.

I loved teasing my best friend Susan.

"A strange encounter? I can't wait; I'll be right over. Bye." Susan hung up the phone.

I just stared down at my phone, shrugged and put it back into my pocket. Driving home I was getting a weird feeling about this violin. I tried looking out my back window, but it was raining so hard I could not see if I was being followed or not.

2

ARRIVING HOME I parked in the street,
grabbed my violin and ran through the rain to my side
door.

Woof woof woof, slurp slurp.

I'm so happy your home, Sophie. Oops, I tinkled.

"Kanani, down girl, ha ha, come on you need to
go out. Let me put this on the table."

My dog was happy to see me, and I was happy to
see her too.

I put down the violin on the little table by the
back door and let Kanani outside. Then I went back to
clean up her mess. I just finished, and she was jumping
up on the door looking in the window. She didn't like
to be outside without me for very long. Lol.

I let her in and she ran over to the refrigerator
and stared at it thumping her tail.

I'm hungry now, Sophie.

I looked at her and laughed.

"Let me get my wet clothes off and I'll feed you,
Kanani."

She then followed me into my bedroom. I got
my damp clothes off, put on stretch jeans and a
sweatshirt. Then I braided my dark blond hair. I was

just finishing up when Susan came through the front door holding her umbrella in one hand and pizza in the other.

"Hi Susan, you can just put it on the counter. I will be right there." I said.

"Hi Sophie."

Kanani ran out of the bedroom and over to greet Susan.

Hi Susan.

"Hi Kanani." Thump thump thump.

Susan put the pizza on top of the oven and pet Kanani.

Oh, I like that. Kanani said.

What another violin?" Susan asked me.

"It involves my strange encounter I mentioned," I told her walking over to it and opening it up.

"I can't wait to hear about it, let me open some wine and pour us each a glass." Susan did that and walked back over to look inside with me.

"Hmm, some lady came in before closing and left this with me, saying it is from my grandfather and I would understand. My grandfather is always up to some adventure or something mysterious, but this is strange indeed. I have lost track of where he is at the moment. Unless he joined a monastery like he always talked about doing after Grandma died." I told Susan, taking out the violin. I searched through the case. Nothing, I looked inside the violin. It didn't have a name. I put my finger through the hole and felt around.

"There's something in here."

"Sophie, don't you still have your luthier tools?

"Yes, I'm sure I brought them with me when we left Hawaii. Let me go check." I looked for Kanani. She was staring at the pizza.

"Let me feed Kanani first, before she devours our pizza, Susan."

I walked over to the fridge and took out Kanani's food placing it in front of her. Then I walked into my bedroom and looked in the closet. I came out carrying my tools. It had been a long time since I had used them. In fact, these tools are the same ones Grandpa had before he gave them to me and taught me how to use them to make the violin I play all the time. I picked up the violin; took it out of the case and set it down on the table. I took off the strings, popped the top off with my trusty little tool.

"Hmmm, I don't know if I just ruined the violin." Then I saw something!

"Look, Susan! An envelope is taped on the inside of it."

"Wow that was clever Sophie. What's in it?"

"Thanks," I replied. "Let's see."

I carefully removed the envelope and placed the top back on without securing it. Then I put the violin back in its case. I would have to deal with that later.

"Let's get our pizza and wine then go sit by the fireplace and read this."

"Ok, I'll grab the pizza and make the fire." Susan told me. She placed the pizza on the coffee table and walked over starting the fire.

I grabbed the wine and turned the TV on low, then sat on the couch. Susan joined me a few minutes later.

"Ok, let's see what it's in the letter," I told Susan with excitement. My hands were shaking as I unfolded the letter. I began reading:

"My dear Sophia, I have sent you this message because time is of the essence for you to accomplish what I am asking of you.

I have made a decision to enter the Trappist Monks in Begrolles-en-Maugges. This is in Western France, not far from Normandy. I am extremely happy about this decision and I have turned all my property over to you. You must go to Le Mont Michel in France; in a vault you will find the Stradivarius Violin. It is essential you get this violin and prove to the world that you are the rightful heir. The sooner you do this the safer you will be. I am sorry but leaving this to you has already put you in grave danger. Monsieur Gaspard must be exposed and arrested as soon as possible. He wants this violin and will stop at nothing to get it. All will be revealed when you enter the vault located in the village by the Church in Le Mont Michel, France. You will also discover our real heritage, a story you have never known. Not even your dear father had the opportunity to find out the truth before his early death. You must be very careful.

My father hid the Stradivarius during World War ll from the Nazis in Le Mont St. Michel. He received it from his father, and his father received it from his father. You get the idea; it has been in our family since 1690 when it was made.

I am going to give you some hints to attain the passwords to enter this vault. You will find a hint in Austria at the Eagles Nest. You must look out over the mountains at sunset. Read Psalm 107, what you find at the Eagles Nest is in this Psalm.

To enter the first vault, you need to memorize 2012stradivariussophia and destroy this letter. God speed my love and know that I am praying for you and will the rest of my life."

I Love You,

Grandpa

I put the letter down and looked at Susan; her eyes were wide with astonishment. I could not believe what I just read.

"I can't believe this Sophia."

"Me either," I replied getting up. "Let's look up that Psalm."

"Sophia, look." Susan pointed at the television.

I stopped and turned around, then went over and turned up the volume. The reporter was saying:

"There has been an accident in Coupeville tonight at the ferry: There was gunfire and a woman named Rachael McFarland was shot; then she disappeared. We don't know the extent of her injuries. There are torrential winds with heavy rain; the police have closed the ferry for the rest of the evening."

The wind was whipping through the reporters' hair and he was having a hard time keeping his balance. As he was trying to finish his report, the power went out!

3

"OH NO!" I exclaimed. "This is just awful! First of all, what did Grandpa mean by I'll know who I am. You know who I am, we've been friends for ten years. This doesn't make any sense. Actually, it's a bit insane." I looked at Susan in exasperation. I was getting myself upset.

"I don't know, it's really weird, Sophia, but things always happen to you and you bounce out of it. This one just might top the other adventures though." Susan was laughing.

Her laughter was contagious, and I started laughing as well.

"Very funny. Ok, I'm supposed to destroy this letter. I don't want to but know I should." I was trying to convince myself to destroy the letter.

"Can you help me remember the combination?" I asked Susan.

"Yes, I can, it's 2012stradivariussophia. We need to go to the Eagle's Nest in Austria, read Psalm 107 first, then on to France. I don't get what word in Psalm 107 we need to memorize tough, it's a bit mysterious. " she said.

"Ok, I'm convinced you have the key components memorized, thank you."

With that I flung it into the fire. I was excited to tell John about this, but we needed to take care of ourselves at the moment.

"Let me get some flashlights, it's getting dark." I walked over to the kitchen and opened a drawer, pulling out two flashlights. I turned them on.

"They both work. Take these Susan while I find some votive candles."

She walked over and took the flashlights while I grabbed four candles and some matches.
Then I joined her on the couch. Kanani curled up next to me.

"Let's sit here for a bit and talk, then I guess you should stay over tonight." I said.

"Yes, I don't want to go home while the power is out." Susan replied.

"I have extra night clothes for you. I need to get my phone and try to call John." I said getting up. Kanani followed me into the bedroom. I grabbed my phone and pulled out some night clothes for Susan then walked back out to the living room and sat on the couch.

"Here's some bed clothes." I said handing them to her.

"Thank you, Sophie." she said.

I looked at my phone.

"Oh no, there's no reception and it needs charging." I said.

"Let me get my phone and try, Sophie." Susan walked over to her coat and pulled out her phone. I don't have any reception either. She stuck it in her pocket then walked back over and sat down.

"I'm worried about that Rachael person. she's the one that brought me the violin. Grandpa said in his letter that I would be in danger, you didn't see anything else in this case did you Susan?" I asked her.

"No, Sophia, you went through it really well and then you destroyed the letter, so you are ok." She said getting up from the couch.

"Well let's clean up and get ready for bed, come on Kanani, outside one more time tonight," I said walking over to the door letting her out.

"Whew, is it still nasty out!" I told Susan.

"I know, its dark out too, no moon," she replied.

I let Kanani back in and we all went to bed. I tossed and turned thinking about that letter and what it could mean to me, actually to all of us. I wished John was here or we were all back in Hawaii.

Woof! Woof! Kanani barked as she jumped off my bed. It woke me with a start. I reached for my lamp but there was still no power, so I grabbed my flashlight.

Woof! Woof! Woof! This is serious Sophie, let me out there! Kanani kept barking and trying to open the bedroom door.

She must have heard Susan getting up to use the bathroom. I opened up the door and Kanani rushed out growling and barking.

"Susan? Is that you?" I called out, there was no answer.

It was cold in the living room and wind was coming in from somewhere.

"Who's there?" I shouted. There was still no answer, all I heard was some scuffling.

Kanani bit someone! I heard a scream! Someone bolted out the front door with her running after them.

I ran to the door and almost slipped on something. I looked down, Kanani had ripped a big chunk out of some ones' raincoat. I ran outside and called out, "Kanani, let him go, come back, now!"

She turned around, thank goodness, and came back into the house. I shoved the piece of clothing out of the way and tried to push the door closed. The wind was so strong I couldn't shut it.

"Sophia? "What's happening?" Susan came running out of her room.

"Please help me shut this door. Someone broke in here tonight, Kanani bit them and he went out screaming."

She came running over and with her help we got the door closed, then I moved the flashlight all around the room.

"The violin is gone!" I yelled running over to the table.

"Someone is on to us!" I exclaimed. "Grandpa was right; we are in danger now!"

4

"LET'S WAIT until daylight, I'll get packed. We can go to your house, so you can pack too. Then let's get to the Seattle Airport and fly to Austria!" I exclaimed.

"Great plan, another adventure for us." Susan said with a bit of anxiety.

"I have to find Kanani's service pack, so she can sit with us on the plane." I walked into the hall closet. Found it and brought it out.

"Let's try our cell phones again. I know it's three hours earlier in Hawaii, but maybe we can get a text out to the boys." I went into the bedroom and grabbed my cell phone from the nightstand.

"Darn, I still can't get a text message to go out! I know John and Kimo are really worried. My phone needs charging too. I should have charged it at work today before the power went out." I told Susan.

"I know they're worried Sophia. Let's get my phone." She ran into the bedroom retrieving her phone. Susan was in there a long time before she came out and said, "I turned off my phone to save the power and it's charged sixty percent. However, I don't have any bars either. I'm sure they've heard about the weather we're having. I just hope the Hood Canal

Bridge is not closed when we get there."

"Well at least you have your phone charged. Thank you for doing that. I hope the bridge is open too," I said.

I got packed, loaded Kanani into the car and we drove to Susan's house. She ran inside while I waited in the car with Kanani. I glanced up and down the street. Nothing looked suspicious, but I wasn't sure. Susan came out a short time later and threw her bag into the car. She jumped in the passenger seat, and then we drove out of Port Townsend. The wind was blowing really hard. I was having trouble keeping the car on the road. The rain was still coming down turning into hail.

"Why did we leave Hawaii Susan? Can you refresh my memory?" I asked her wistfully.

"You wanted a change of scenery after having your yacht stolen and market burned to the ground," Susan replied. "Then we all agreed with you and moved here."

"Yes, I do remember," I answered. "Sorry."

"It's ok Sophie; this is the first bad thing that's happened in a whole year!" Susan tried to cheer me up.

We got to the Hood Canal Bridge; it was closed because of the wind.

"Darn! I wonder how long this will be closed." I said to Susan and Kanani. Looking thoughtfully out the window wishing it was just a submarine holding up the bridge.

"Let me see if my phone works here," Susan said picking up her phone. "I have one bar; I'll try to send out a text to Kimo. What do you want me to say?" Susan asked me.

"Tell him we are on our way to Austria. Also, we would like both John and him to meet us at the Eagles Nest in Austria or Saint Monte Michel in France. Let him know that we are going to Austria first though. Please tell him my phone needs charging so I haven't been able to get ahold of John. Hmm, better tell him that we are going, because I received a mysterious message from my grandfather. Don't mention the danger, because that will just worry both of them. Tell him Kanani is with us, that should suffice I think. Can you think of anything I've missed?" I asked.

"No, I got everything you said and I'm hitting send. It went! Now let me call the airport and check on flights."

"That's great it went, Susan. Ok, I hope you get through before we start driving and you lose service."

"I'm getting through and they're answering, just a minute Sophie."

"Hello." Susan made the reservations.

The bridge opened, and we were on our way.

We boarded the plane and sat in first class.

Kanani was allowed in with me, I let out a sigh of relief. I kept looking around to make sure no one was watching us. Surely Grandpa was exaggerating about real danger. I was sleepy and decided to take a nap.

Susan nudged me, I woke up, "Sophie," she whispered in my ear, "There are two men watching us. I went to the restroom and one followed me. I had to hide in there until the stewardess knocked on the door to see if I was ok. She walked me back to my seat."

"Where are they?" I whispered back.

She turned her head to the side and nodded to the left a bit, "over there."

I looked behind us and there were two men. One was short and stocky with a blond ponytail. The other looked scraggly with a dark beard, dark hair and very tall. When they saw me looking at them, they both looked away.

"Well, we just need to keep an eye on them," I told her.

"When we land, we'll rent a car and find a place to stay in town. I'm feeling a bit uncomfortable; we must be on our guard. I couldn't carry my gun on the plane, not that I ever carry it anyway." I added.

"I know Sophie. I'm feeling a bit scared."

"Well at least we have Kanani. I believe she bit the intruder last night. I think that stocky one over there is the one that broke into the house. Thinking about that gives me the creeps," I said with a shiver.

"I wish the guys were here, you know maybe we should have waited for them to return from Hawaii." Susan replied.

"I'm feeling the same way Susan. I'm getting a really uneasy feeling. I need to get up and walk around. I'll be right back." I motioned for Kanani to stay.

Getting up, I stepped over Susan and walked past the two men. They acted like they were ignoring me. I looked back and saw they were keeping track of what I was doing. I walked to the back of the plane and looked out. Several people were talking, so I joined them.

"Hi, where are you from," I asked a nicely dressed woman next to me.

"Hi, I am from Salzburg, I'm returning home from visiting my son and his family in Seattle. Where are you going?" she asked me.

"I'm on my way to Austria. I'm with my friend and dog, we are going to see the Eagle's Nest. I was there as a child with my grandfather and have a desire to go back to Salzburg," I told her.

"Well, you will enjoy it. You will see why I live in such a beautiful place and have never left. I am going to return to my seat now, nice meeting you, have a wonderful vacation."

"Goodbye, nice meeting you too," I told her as she walked away.

Someone bumped into me. I turned around and looked. I was face to face with a young, medium sized man. He had blond hair and was wearing designer jeans and a leather jacket.

He looked at me and said, "Sorry, I tripped over that toy a child left in the aisle. I hope I didn't hurt you."

He pointed at a toy car. Then he bent over and picked it up returning it to the child in the seat to the left of him.

"That's ok, I'm fine." I told him, and then I walked back to my seat.

When I returned, Susan was happy to have me back for company. Kanani was too. Susan looked really uneasy.

"Anything happen?" Susan asked me.

"Not really, I just met a woman going home to Austria after visiting her family in Seattle." I gave Kanani a pat on the head. I skipped telling her about the young man.

Just then the stewardess came by with the food cart.

"Do you want chicken or beef," asked the stewardess.

"I will take two chicken dinners," I said pointing at Kanani.

"I will have chicken too," Susan told her.

After eating, the trays were picked up and the

movie was turned off. I opened the blinds and looked out the window. I saw the mountains and Salzburg; we were getting close to landing.

"Susan, look down there," I moved so she could look out.

"Wow, what a beautiful city," Susan said, her eyes getting big. "Too bad it isn't a vacation for us," she added reflectively.

"Susan, we must pretend it is just that, a vacation. Still we must be very careful and on guard." We prepared for landing.

5

AFTER GOING through customs, we walked over to the car rental and leased a Mini Cooper. We loaded Kanani in first and then the luggage. We ventured off towards the town center.

"Look Susan, there's the "Top Hotel Mozart," I said pointing my finger to the right.

"I read about it on the plane, let's see if we can stay there with Kanani. They have an Internet café and room service. I need to do some research on Le Monte St. Michel, read Psalm 107 and then we need to get in touch with the boys. Does that sound like a good plan?" I asked her.

"Yes, very good, if you stop in front I'll run in and see if they allow dogs," Susan replied.

I pulled in front of the hotel. It was nice, I hoped they allowed dogs and had an opening.

Susan came back out a bit later.

"Can we stay here?" I asked hopefully.

"Yes, I booked a double room. We can drop our bags here with the bellman and they'll park our car," she said.

"Great news, that'll make me fill more secure," I told her.

Once in the room I plugged in my phone and

checked it for text messages.

"John sent me a text; they're on the next flight out of Hawaii to Salzburg. They'll land at ten thirty tomorrow night. I'm going to text him that we'll pick them up. We need to go early and trade in our car for something bigger or someone will be sitting in the trunk," I laughed.

"Ha ha, that's funny. Did he give you the flight number?" Susan asked laughing at my joke.

"Yes, I have it," I read it off to her. "Let's tour the city tomorrow; how about starting at Mozart's residence." I was reading the travel guide to her.

"We could take the Salzburg City tour by bus; and see Mozart's birthplace and all of the major sites. Kanani would have to spend two hours in the room. Then we could come get her. She can go to St. Peter's Monastery with us, which is a Benedictine Abbey. It's been in existence since the Seventh century! How about that Susan? What do you think?" I asked her looking up from the brochure.

"Sounds like fun. However, now that the boys are coming here tomorrow night; I think we should see some sites with them too. It's a good cover and will drive those guys following us crazy!" she said.

"I agree, however, we need to be worried about them and on guard. They seem serious about getting the information I have."

"True, Sophie, I didn't mean it to sound like I'm

not worried." Susan said.

"I know," Sophie hugged her.

"I wonder if our men want to go to the salt mines," I asked her.

"I know Kimo would! That sounds like fun, Sophie!" Susan was getting excited, so was I. Kanani barked.

"Why not have some fun; we might just be in for the fight of our lives, again." I told her. "At least we have Kanani to protect us and the men will be with us soon."

"You're right and don't forget John is a black belt in karate."

We had jetlag and very little sleep from the night before, so we fell right to sleep.

It was in the middle of the night that I heard a slight sound. It woke me up. Kanani was growling, I reached for the lamp and turned on the light. I snuck over to the door to have a look. There was an intruder in the living room. He was one of the men from the plane; he was rummaging through my suitcase!

"Hey, what do you think you're doing, get out of my room," I shouted at him running over to grab it from him.

Kanani zoomed past me and grabbed his leg, ripping a piece of his pants off. He screamed and threw a book at me from the coffee table. I dodged and he missed. Then he took out a gun and aimed it at

Kanani.

"Get your mutt off me or I'll shoot her," he said glaring at me.

6

"KANANI, LET GO!" I frantically cried. I was terrified he was going to shoot her. She let go and came over to me. "Good girl," I hugged her, "I love you."

I love you too, but I could make him go away, Sophie. Kanani just looked at me.

"Now, don't move or you'll be sorry," He said as he dumped my clothes out on the floor. Then he grabbed my suitcase and bolted out the door. I ran over to the door just in time to see him disappear down the hall.

Boy I want to chase that man. Kanani looked up at Sophie and sat down next to her.

"Sophia," yelled Susan running out of her room barefoot, "what happened?"

"Someone broke in and then took off with my suitcase and some clothes," I said picking up the pieces not stolen.

"That's weird." she said. "Should we call hotel security?"

"That's an excellent idea. This whole thing is getting weirder and more dangerous by the minute." I ran over to the phone.

"Security will be right up, Susan. Get a robe on, I'll go get mine."

All three of us waited in the living room for security. Five minutes later there was a knock on the door.

Kanani barked. *Be careful Sophie, I'm going over there with you!*

I looked through the keyhole and saw the security officer standing outside our door, so I opened it.

We both gave our statements.

"We will keep a watch out for this man you described. I'll have this floor watched tonight. I suggest you move to another hotel in the morning and go to the police." he said.

"Thank you for helping us. We feel better knowing hotel security is watching this floor. We'll discuss what we're going to do in the morning. Good night." I said.

With that he got up and left us.

I walked back over to Susan and sat down.

"I have an idea; I am going to go buy two RV's, one for you and Kimo, the other for John, Kanani and me. That way we can use them to travel and we don't have to stay in hotels where someone can rob us. I wanted to use the computer center, but I'm going to go buy an Apple computer at the shopping center across the street. Afterwards I need to replace the clothes stolen out of my suitcase. Then we'll have everything we need. Do you think that is a good idea, Susan?"

"Wow, that was a lot of thinking you just did, but it is a good plan and I like it," Susan replied sitting on the couch pulling her robe over her.

"Do you think we should forget about being tourists today?" she asked me.

"Yes I do, what time is it?" I asked her.

"Let me look. It's three a.m.," Susan replied. "What the heck, we're on vacation. Do you want a glass of wine?" I asked her walking over to the mini bar.

"Sure, why not, I can't sleep either." Susan said as she took the glass of wine from me. I sat down on the couch next to her.

After we calmed down I went back to bed with Kanani, Susan curled up on the couch.

I won't sleep Sophie, you and Susan will be safe tonight. Kanani was soon fast asleep because I heard her snoring.

I woke up at seven a.m., not too rested from our night's adventure. Kanani looked rested. Susan was still out like a light on the couch. I told Kanani to be quiet and then I jumped into the shower, afterwards putting on one of my blue no wrinkle dresses.

"Come on Kanani, let's not wake up Susan and I'll take you out girl." I snapped a leash on her and we quietly left the room.

Whew, that was close. I needed to out.

Kanani must really have had to go, I thought.

When we walked back into the hotel, I went into the café and ordered breakfast to be delivered to our room.

Did you order enough for me too Sophie? Kanani looked up at Sophie.

"Oh, yes, please add an order of scrambled eggs and a hamburger patty to that order." I told the waitress.

That's better. Kanani thumped her tail.

After that Kanani and I went into a shop. I bought some clothes to replace the missing outfits and a travel bag. When we walked into the room Susan had just gotten out of the shower. She looked refreshed dressed in a skirt, t-shirt and sneakers.

"Good morning Susan, I have breakfast coming in half an hour. That gives us time to pack."

"Good morning, Sophie, I hope today is better than last night," she replied.

"Me too."

After breakfast we left the room,
I carried my bag and Susan carried out her suitcase. We took off in the Mini to look for RV dealerships.

"There's a dealership, Sophia," Susan pointed to the sign on the left side of the road up ahead.

I pulled in and we parked in front of the building. As we got out of the car a tall man in a dark suit walked out to greet us. Kanani had her head out the window watching us.

"Hallo, guten morgen," he said.

"Guten morgen," I replied. "Sprichst du Englishch?"

"Ich spreche ein bisschen Englishch," he said.

Then continued with, "entschuldigen sie bitte," turned and walked back into the shop.

"What did you two just say Sophia," Susan asked me.

"He said good morning and then I asked him if he spoke English; he replied that he spoke a little bit of English. Then he said, excuse me before he turned around and left us."

I looked up; another man was walking out to greet us. He was a bit shorter and plumper than the first man, also wearing a dark suit.

"Good morning, my name is Jacob Astor," he said coming out of the door and down the steps to shake my hand.

"Good morning. My name is Sophia Anderson, this is my friend Susan Kai and my dog Kanani," I said shaking his hand. At least we had someone that spoke good English.

"We need to look at RV's, I want to buy two small ones."

"Do you need financing?" he asked me.

"No, I'll pay cash," I told him.

"Well, we have many different styles. If you are going to drive through little towns in Europe you should buy two small ones. Otherwise you cannot go everywhere. There are a lot of narrow roads." he replied showing us a Winnebago. We finally settled on two small Winnebago's.

We hooked up the car to my Winnebago and Susan followed me in the other RV. I had already bought the computer, so now we were off to a super store to shop. We loaded the RV's with bedding, towels, dishes and food. Then we took the Mini back and exchanged it for a Volkswagen Passat. Finishing that we found a campground and checked in.

"Susan, it is only three p.m., let me take Kanani for a walk. Afterwards would you like to go with me for a drive through the town?" I asked.

"Yes, that would be fun. We owe it to ourselves to relax a bit. By the time you two are back, I'll be ready."

We drove into Salzburg and stopped for a quick tour of Wolfgang Amadeus Mozart's house.

"Look, Susan, the first violin Mozart ever played at the age of five!" I was amazed with all of the instruments they had on exhibit.

"What make of violin is it Sophie?" asked Susan.

"It's a Steiner, I read somewhere that his father cautioned him about playing a Stradivarius, because it was considered "orchestral" instruments in Austria and

Germany during that time of his life.

After touring his house, we left to go eat. Then we headed to the airport to pick up the guys that were flying in from Hawaii. The plane landed a few minutes late, I had butterflies in my stomach. We had to wait another half hour for them to go through customs.

"Here they are Susan!" I yelled running over to hug John.

"Sophie," John said giving me a hug. He was dressed in a Hawaiian shirt, khaki pants, and loafers. He had just shaved and his dark hair was cut short, he smelled like aftershave.

"Kimo, I am so glad you're here," cried Susan then threw her arms around his neck.

Kimo was also in a Hawaiian shirt, black pants, and loafers. He was a bit broader then John, his hair a bit longer and he had a mustache.

"I am so happy to be here with you girls."said John. "This is all we brought with us so let's go. Please fill us in and don't leave out anything," he added as we walked to side by side to the rental car.

"Susan, what possessed you two to fly over here without us?" Kimo wanted to know.

"You'll understand once we explain everything," I said to both of them.

Susan nodded in agreement.

I added, "there's been a change of plans. Last night we got broken into at the hotel, so we bought two

Winnebago's for us to travel in. We feel safer this way. We're staying in a campground not far from here."

"Your room was broken into?" John asked me, grabbing my arm and pulling me around to look at him. His green eyes were serious looking.

"It's a long story. Let's get in the car and I will tell it the best I can with Susan's help."

He let go shaking his head and followed me to the car. Once we were on our way, I began the story.

"Susan please jump in here and help with anything I've missed," I told her as I resumed my tale.

"Ok, but you are doing a great job by yourself, Sophia." she said.

The whole story was told before we arrived at the Winnebago's.

Kimo looked at both of us and said, "we really can't leave you two alone; every time we do something happens."

"I know it seems that way," I told him unlocking the front door.

"Come in and let's have a bite to eat and something to drink."

"Ok, sounds like a plan," Kimo replied.

Kanani jumped all over John and Kimo with licks and hugs.

John, Kimo, I've missed you. I'm so excited.

"Hi Kanani, you're taking good care of your

mommy, good girl," John told her. We sat down around the table with Kanani sitting on my feet.

"Ok, who wants, wine, beer or tea?" I asked.
Everyone wanted a glass of wine, so I opened up a bottle and poured four glasses. Then sat the bottle on the counter placing crackers and cheese out too. We had a nice evening.

The next morning we got up and after breakfast, decided to take the RV's to Berchtesgaden. We dropped off the Passat at the airport first, though.

"Look John, there's a campsite," I said pointing to left.

"Let me pull in there and then we can see if they have any space available," John answered.

John pulled our RV in and Kimo pulled theirs in behind us. I got out of ours and went over to talk to Susan. John and Kimo went into the office of Campsite Allweglehen Berchtesgaden. Coming out rather quickly, they both had grins on their faces.

"So sorry, no empty places tonight," said Kimo mischievously.

"Ok, wipe the grin off your face Kimo," Susan said laughing. "You're playing with us, where do we park?"

"Follow me, my dear," Kimo said as he grabbed her hand to show her the choices.

"John, you two are a delight to have around," I told him, as he grabbed my hand grinning. We picked out a spot under a tree with gorgeous views of the mountains.

Moving both Winnebago's into their spots, I took Kanani out and walked her around the grounds. Kanani sniffed every tree and ran around with delight.

I love camping. Whew, I smell a boar somewhere. Let me find it.

"Kanani, come on. I had to tug her away from a bush to get her moving.

When we returned, Susan had placed a lunch spread out for us on the picnic table.

"This is so nice! Thank you Susan," I said hugging her.

"Isn't it lovely being here Sophia?" Susan asked me.

"Yes, the best," I told her sitting down next to her.

During lunch we made plans to go up to the Eagle's Nest that afternoon.

"Sophia, did you look up Psalm 107 yet? Susan asked me.

"Yes, I did, it is about God, a refuge in all dangers. The first word is *alleluia!* That must be what I need to see up at the Eagle's Nest. Something that makes me feel alleluia." I finished saying.

"Well we shall see Sophie," said John affectionately.

"I can't wait Sophie," Susan said cleaning up the

rest of the lunch from the table and dumping it in the trash.

"Come, Kanani, you need to stay in the Winnebago and protect it. Be a good girl and we will see you when we return," I told her petting her on the head. I grabbed my jacket running out to join the others.

Don't leave me, no! I don't want to stay here. Please please take me with you? Kanani was whining, it made me feel bad.

It was a short walk over to the busses; we boarded one and started the long scary drive up to the Eagle's Nest.

"I would hate to fall off this road!" I said nervously to John.

"Me too, you can't have a fear of heights coming up here." he said to calm my fears.

Susan and Kimo got on the bus behind us. There wasn't room on the one we were on. Plus, we thought it was a good plan for us to spread out. We never knew when these men were going to show up and try something else with us.

"Look at that view! It's called the "Hoher Goli," isn't it magnificent?" I said to John.

"Yes it is," he answered. "This is an adventurous bus ride and the view is like a fairy tale. How did you know that?"

"I looked it up," I told him grinning.

Getting off the bus, I gasped, "oh, it's hard to breathe."

"Just take it slow honey," John told me as he took my arm. "Let's go over to the elevators and wait for Kimo and Susan, then you can sit down a bit."

"Sounds good to me, I think it's just the altitude. Although the beauty of this place takes my breath away too, literally." I said half-jokingly.

Sitting down on a bench we waited for Kimo and Susan to arrive, I was getting my breath back.

"There they are," I said jumping up. "Hi guys, what did you think of that bus ride?"

"It's a bit scary driving up here," Susan said walking over to me.

John got up, "I'll be right back. Let me see if we need tickets to get on the elevator." He walked over to the terminal.

Coming back, John said, "ok, we don't need any more tickets, the bus tickets will do. Should we get in line?"

Standing up I said, "yes, let's do it!"

Susan got up with me and we all walked over to the elevators. It was a terrifying ride up. It was five thousand feet above the ground. All passengers were told to step out at the top. We were on the balcony overlooking the mountains.

"John, can you guys pose over there? I want to take a snap shot?" I asked him as I pointed to a spot with gorgeous mountains in the background.

"Yes, and then I want one of us too." he said.

"We'll get all sorts of photos of us," I told him with a big grin on my face. He grinned back at me.

We took tons of photos. Then we went on the tour. It ended in the café; we sat down for a meal as the altitude and exertion was making us hungry. The sun was setting and I was getting chilly, so I put on my jacket and got up from the table.

"I need to go have a look outside," I told everyone.

"We're coming with you," Susan said. Susan, John and Kimo got up and followed me out.

"Ok, hurry I'm excited," I told them. I was looking for an angel in the mountains that was praising God. We looked out over the mountains. It was light enough to see the view.

"Look!" I said pointing, "there's a statue of an angel. His wings are out, his arms are reaching above him and his face is looking up to Heaven. He looks like he is praising God."

"Wow, that's incredible, look down there. There's another angel doing the same thing below us." John said.

I glanced down and there was another one. That angel was holding a book up above his head.

"Sophia," said Kimo, "There's one to the right of us too. This one's on his knees praying."

"This is so amazing; I have never seen anything like this in my life!" I told all of them.

"Me either, I am glad we came here," Susan said with a warm smile.

"It's incredible," Kimo and John both said at the same time. They looked over at each other and laughed.

The sun was down too far now to see anymore, so we went back inside and ordered dessert.

"I think it's a good idea to take separate busses again," John said.

"I do too," said Kimo. "We should go down after you, to make sure that if anyone is waiting at the bottom we can help you."

"Good idea," John replied. "Come on Sophia let's get this bus," John said taking my hand. We jumped on the next to the last bus of the evening. Quickly, I skimmed people's faces.

"John, look. That's the guy that broke into my hotel room," I pointed over at the man. He was sitting two seats in front of us on the right hand side of the bus. He was looking at me.

"I am going to go talk to him and find out what's going on," John said as he stood up.

I saw him pull out his gun before I could stop John.

"No, John don't! He has a gun!" I screamed too late.

John dodged the bullet; it hit the window next to our seats shattering it. Everyone was panicking. The bus was screeching and twisting down the windy steep mountain path in the dark. We were standing up trying to hold on and not fall down. Some big guy behind me opened the escape door beside him and pulled me back to his seat.

"Ok, hold on to me and jump," he said.

"We're going too fast, I'm scared!" I told him. I was really far more than scared! John ran up behind me.

"Sophie, jump I am right behind you," John yelled in my ear.

I jumped with the stranger holding my hand and John jumped out after us. The bus kept on going down the windy path barely under control. The front of the bus was unaware of what just took place in the back. We hit the ground and rolled into some bushes. I glanced up and saw the man with the gun jump out of the bus down the hill.

He fired at us and started running up the hill in our direction. He shot his gun and it hit the stranger that helped me, in his left leg. I turned around and grabbed his arm.

Turning my head in John's direction I screamed at him. "John, our new friend has been shot!"

I was terrified!

"Let me get him," John said running over and grabbing the guy.

"There's the next bus!" I yelled running into the road. "Sophie, get out of the road!" John was frantically waving his arms to make me move out of the way.

I was waving at the driver of the oncoming bus. He put on his airbrakes; luckily he wasn't going too fast. I jumped out of the way before he hit me. He skidded and came to a stop just beyond us.

He opened his door, "what are you people doing in the road?" the bus driver yelled. "You could be killed out there in the dark!"

"There's someone chasing us, he shot this man in the leg. We were on the bus before you." I shouted so he could hear me.

"Get on!" he yelled back. Then picked up his radio to call the bus we just jumped out of. He told them what had happened and to wait at the bottom for the police. It had gotten itself under control, because we didn't see it stranded along the side of the road.

"Sophie, give me your hand," Kimo said as he rushed up to the door.

He pulled me up into the bus. Everyone was asking what was going on.

They got the wounded guy on the bus and then the driver closed the door and started back down the road.

"Sophie, are you ok?" Susan asked hugging me as I sat down next to her with Kimo standing in the aisle.

"Yes, I'm just shook up a bit," I told her and hugged her back.

"They're getting more than dangerous; why would they shoot at me if they want the code?" I asked her.

"They didn't shoot at you, they want to kidnap you and get rid of anyone else in their way!" Susan said.

I thought about that, "wow, I'm glad they didn't get me," I said.

"I am glad they didn't either," Susan sighed.

When we got to the bottom of the drive, police were waiting for us. We gave statements and then medics fixed up my poor wounded brave hero and took him to the hospital. We thanked him profoundly and exchanged names and numbers. He was a schoolteacher in England and was here on vacation. What a vacation he was having.

"Let's get back to the Winnebago's and regroup," John said.

"Good idea," answered Kimo.

We walked back to the campground, opened our RV door, and found Kanani very upset.

Someone was here. They tried to break in. I was a good dog and didn't let them in. It's a good thing you didn't' take me with you. I'm such a good dog!

"Kanani get down. It's ok, you're a good girl." I told her. She finally stopped jumping up on me.

Look John," I said, "it looks like someone tried to get in the door; Kanani practically shredded the door trying to get at the intruder. Once again Kanani has protected us." I pet Kanani again.

I love ear scratches.

"I see that, I'm glad she's ok. It doesn't look like they're afraid of her, but at least they didn't get in," he said.

"I'll go see if ours is ok," Kimo left and quickly went over to his RV. He checked out the inside.

"Everything looks ok over here," he said as he walked back over to our RV.

"I'll get us some wine," John told all of us. He poured us each a generous serving of wine to calm us down.

"I need something stronger than wine," I said half-jokingly.

"I know, but this all we have." Susan laughed trying to make light of the situation.

"Ok, I think we need to get out of here and on our way to Le Mont St. Michel as soon as possible." I told everyone.

"Me too," said Susan. The boys agreed.

Tomorrow we would be driving to France!

The next morning, we packed up and left Austria,

driving west through the northern tip of Switzerland and entering France at St. Gingolph near dusk. We drove north towards Strasbourg and found a campground on the Rhine River.

"What a breath of fresh air," I said stretching after getting out of the RV.

"Oh, it's beautiful, Sophie," said Susan!

Kanani ran out and jumped into the water. There was a little inlet with a beach. I grabbed some food, John made a fire in the pit and Kimo grabbed the wine.

After eating, we cleaned up and rehashed the last couple of days.

"I am so excited," I said, "tomorrow we should reach Le Mont St. Michel and we will see what's in the vault!"

"I know, it will be hard to sleep tonight," Susan said.

"Well," John said as he stood up. "Kimo and I are going to walk around the campground and make sure no unwanted campers will surprise us tonight."

With that they were gone for about an hour. Susan and I sat around the campfire. Kanani had tired herself out and was lying down by my feet. It wasn't a cold evening, but the fire took off the summer mountain chill.

"Ok, girls we have found the guys that were on the bus including the one that shot at us. They're sleeping in a truck at the front entrance.

We've reported them to the campground office. They are reporting it to the police. I think we should pull out of here in the middle of the night." John told us.

"Oh no, driving in the dark is so dangerous John," I said. "I'm really scared."

"There is nothing to be frightened about with Kimo and me here." John tried to assure me.

"Why don't you girls try to get a bit of rest before we take off tonight?"

"Ok, if I can rest. Come on Susan, come Kanani." I called both of them. With that we walked over to our Winnebago. I rested on my bed with Kanani and Susan slept in the loft.

It seemed like a minute and then John was shaking me.

"Sophie, wake up, it's time to go," he said.

"What time is it John?" I asked with a big yawn.

"Nearly midnight."

"Ok, I'll try to wake up." I got up and put on some coffee for us, letting Kanani out for a quick potty.

Well I guess I could go right now, oh smell that nice night air. Ummm.

"Kanani, come back in dear." I told my darling dog.

She turned around looked at me and came bounding in and then went back to bed.

Kimo woke up Susan too. Then John got into the driver's seat and started the engine.

"Wait," said Susan, "our RV is still here!"

"I know," said Kimo, "I grabbed our clothes and got what we need. We're leaving it as a decoy. We can go faster with one RV."

"Good Idea." Susan replied.

We pulled out the back entrance with the lights off, not even going by the bad guys. John was going to make sure they didn't see us leave. Then instead of heading north towards Le Mont St. Michel, he drove us southwest.

"I'm scared; I hope he got my toothbrush." Susan said trying to stifle a nervous giggle.

"Well, I am scared too. It would be scarier staying here tonight and having those guys follow us all day tomorrow." I told her. "I have an extra toothbrush if Kimo forgot yours, now let's look out and make sure we are not being followed."

We looked for any headlights following us. We didn't see anything; perhaps we got away. We ended up in Orleans, France at five in the morning. John was tired, so we stopped at a café and had breakfast. Kimo drove the rest of the way and John slept. A few hours later we ended up in Normandy, the home of Le Mont St. Michel.

I looked around; it was like something out of a fairy tale. The parking lot was connected to a walk way and that was connected to the island which contained a village with shops, housing and hotels. At the very top of the village there was the magnificent Cathedral. In history, this was a place that was cut off from the rest of the world in the one hundred years war. The new walkway had been put in within the last thirty years to accommodate the large tourist industry. Years ago people would get stranded at Mont St. Michel's and not be able to get to their car until the tide went back down. This was a unique place and the only place on earth remotely like it was in Cornwall, England. There you have to watch the tide, because you can get stranded on the island for hours. Years ago I had gone there with my sister Jennie. We ran through the water and made it to shore before the tide kept us captive on the island.

"Here is the plan, let's park this Winnebago in the lot then check into a hotel inside the wall," John suggested.

"Great idea," I answered.

"Grab your things girls," said Kimo, "you too Kanani."

John stepped outside the RV and looked around. Then leaned back in and said, "ok, I don't see the bad guys car. Let's go and find some hotel rooms."

We grabbed our things and started walking across the inlet. John and Kimo kept looking behind us. Finally we entered the walled community. It was packed with people pushing and trying to get from one shop then another. John was leading and then Kimo,

Susan, Kanani and I took the rear.

"Here is the first hotel, La Vielle Auberge, I'll run in and check for availability," John ran inside and quickly returned. "They're all booked, let's try the next one."

"This one is Hotel Du Monton Blanc. Say some prayers ladies," John said as he went inside with Kimo.

Kimo came out grinning, so I knew we got some rooms.

"They had three cancellations, so I booked all three rooms for two nights," said John.

"Why all three," I asked.

"So our friends don't check in the same hotel. You must be tired, Sophie, or you would have gotten that," John teased me then gave me a hug and kiss.

"I'm tired," I told him.

We went into the rustic rooms and I looked around. The walls were made of stone and the furnishings were antique. We took a nap for three hours and afterwards cleaned up then meet in the dining room. Sitting by the fireplace we had bread, cheese, cold chicken, and wine.

Chewing on a piece of bread I said, "I called and we can get into the vault at ten a.m. tomorrow morning."

"I am so excited, Sophie," said Susan. "It will be hard to wait until tomorrow."

"I know. After we finish dinner, let's take a walk through the village and up to the church. Maybe we can find where the vault is located and be ready for tomorrow. Plus there are tons of shops," I added excitedly.

"Well, let's hurry and eat so we can go," Susan said as she waved for the waitress.

Kimo and John just shook their heads laughing.

"We need to be careful girls, we don't want these guys to see us tonight and know where we're staying." John said.

"I know, we'll be careful. But I just cannot go back into the room right now and do nothing. Let's get Kanani and take a walk. Plus, I bet they know about the vault," I said. "Especially since Monsieur Gaspard wants the Stradivarius and has been looking for it for years."

"I don't understand your grandfather," said John. "He knew the danger he was putting you in. This better be worth it."

"It will be worth it," I told him reassuringly. We went to the room and put on Kanani's leash so she could go with us. Then we walked all the way up to the church and made it back to our rooms with no problems.

The next morning we arrived at the vault on time. There was an outer door that we went into, which led us into a short hallway. We stopped in front of that door; I had a code that needed to be put in for us to enter.

"Ok, here goes. I'm so nervous I'm shaking," I told everyone.

"It's ok, Sophie, but which code do you use?" Susan asked me.

"Let me try *2012stradivariussophia,*" I typed the letters into the keyboard and out popped a key!

"Yahoo!" I yelled jumping for joy.

"Sophie, calm down. Let me put the key in the door." John said as he took the key out of my hand and put it into the lock.

The heavy door swung open. We walked through shutting it behind us. We were standing in a large vault. I looked around. There were five steel doors on my right and six on my left.

"How do I know which door is ours?" I asked everyone.

"Sophie, remember your grandfather said Psalm 107," Susan told me. "Look over there at that door." She pointed to a door on the right towards the end.

I walked over and looked; at the top in tiny letters was P107.

"This must be it," I said as I went up to the keyboard.

I typed in *alleluia,* nothing happened. Then I tried *angel,* nothing happened.

"Oh, no, I wonder how many chances I get?"

"Try halleluiah," said Susan.

I was shaking so bad I could hardly type it in.

"Ok, here goes," I typed in *halleluiah* and the keyboard opened up. Inside were two keys.

"Should I take them both out?" I asked John looking up at him.

"They look like duplicates, I would leave one in honey," said John. "That way you can get back in here if you misplace this key."

"Ok," I said as I grabbed one key and closed it back up.

I inserted the key in the lock, turned the handle and opened the door. I felt along the wall and found a switch on the right. Turning on the lights, I moved over for everyone to enter and then John closed the door.

"There's a violin case," I said running over to it. Opening it up a letter fell out, but there was no violin. I had a lump in my throat and quickly opened the letter reading it aloud.

"Dear Sophia, if you are reading this, you made it half way."

"Half way," I exclaimed in horror!

"It's ok, Sophie, keep reading." John tried to soothe me.

"A bit of information about Pierre Gaspard, he

lives up to his name sake. Gaspard means treasure bearer in French. This man has been after the one treasure he has not been able to get his hands on. He has been waiting for an opportunity to get it; he thought this would be his chance. Because you are reading this, I know he has failed so far.

400 million Euros and the deed to my estate are in a Swiss Bank. Here is the bank address and account number. The violin is in a vault at the mansion, which I am giving to you. The mansion is located in Luxembourg. It is outside the town of Echternach, the address is 2 Rue de la Blanc.

The keys to the estate and bank safe are inside this envelope. I must tell you that the violin is your heritage, my dear. Our last name is Stradivarius, not Anderson. During World War II my father changed our name for safety sake. This vault you are in now belongs to you as well; you may use it for whatever you want. I have also put 400 million Euros into a Swiss Bank account for your sister, here is her account number. You are the signer on it, since I cannot keep track of her whereabouts.

I know this is a shock to you, but I know you will do good works with this money. Watch out for Monsieur Gaspard and the people he employees. Never give him what he is after, you must declare to the world who you are. This is the only thing that can keep you safe, unless something happens to him.

I love you Sophia, I am happy with what I have done with my life. Perhaps you could honor me someday with a book about the story of my life. I have left extensive notes for you in the vault at home."

Love,

Robert Anderson Stradivarius

I shook the envelope; out fell a big gold key and a small key.

"Wow, I am speechless," I said sitting down on the floor of the vault.

"Sophia, WOW," said John sitting down next to me with his arm around my shoulders. "I guess you should be speechless, I am."

"This is like a fairy tale," said Susan sitting down on my left putting her arm around me too.

"Ok, let's make sure these keys are safe and this letter too, Sophie," said Kimo.

"That is a good idea," said John. "I think you should give me the envelope and keys. Monsieur Gaspard still has his thugs chasing us."

I agreed and handed everything over to John. He safely tucked it inside a closed pocket of his pants that could not be seen.

We left the vault then walked out to the main door and closed that door behind us too. It was such a beautiful day, I could have just sat on the wall and soaked up some sun reflecting on all of the news I had just received. The others must have gone ahead of me. All of a sudden I was grabbed from behind. Someone put their hand on my mouth to stop me from screaming, I kicked and tried to fight back, but he drug me kicking around the corner of the courtyard and down the narrow winding path through the village. Before I knew it we were in the car lot.

8

"SOPHIE, DO YOU want some lunch sweetie?" John asked as he turned around to talk to me.

"Sophie!" screamed John. "Kimo do you see her?"

"There she is up ahead of us; someone is dragging her, run John! Susan keep up," yelled Kimo as they both started running down the narrow cobblestone to the walkway.

Susan was running as fast as she could. Running by the hotel, she hesitated then ran in and got Kanani out of the room. She put on her leash and they both ran back out towards the car lot.

"There she is!" John pointed at me being pushed into a Winnebago. "Why are there two look alike Winnebago's? They must have driven yours here. She is being put into yours! Kimo I'm going to keep following them, here are the keys to the other Winnebago, pick me up on the way out."

"Hey, what do you guys think you're doing taking me like this? What do you want?" I was shouting at them.

"Gag her or put her in the bathroom," growled

the driver. I was roughly grabbed by the arm and shoved into the small bathroom. Banging my knee against the toilet, I caught myself from falling and looked around. This was Susan and Kimo's RV; there was Susan's toothbrush. I could not see behind me and didn't know if John and the gang were following me or not. I prayed they were. If only I had Kanani with me, this would not have happened! I was mad at myself and still in a bit of shock at the letter my grandfather left for me.

We drove about an hour. From what I could see out the bathroom window, we had just entered a village called Le Mans. Suddenly, we stopped and entered through a secured gate; the grounds were beautiful like a botanical garden. In the distance I marveled at the pristine Sarthe River. This mansion was magnificent! It was two stories tall made of white brick with a red cobblestone roof, and the trim was red too. There were balconies off the upper bedrooms with flowerboxes and the gardener was just loading his tools into his truck. It looked like the grounds had just been mowed and the rosebushes trimmed. I could only imagine what the inside looked like. I guess I was about to find out. I wonder what Monsieur Gaspard would be like.

"Get her and bring her in," barked the driver gruffly as he pulled up to the front of the house.

I was grabbed and led out of the RV towards the

ornate double red front doors and taken into a room on the left. I was unceremoniously placed in a chair which rested on the tiled parlor floor.

"No speaking until Monsieur Gaspard greets you. He will arrive soon, would you like some tea?" It was one of the men from the flight over on the plane that asked me. He was the tall one not the one that broke into my hotel room or chased us at the Eagles Nest.

"Yes please, I'm thirsty," I told him looking around at my surroundings. The windows were high, no chance of escape there. The mysterious man left then soon returned.

"Thank you," I said as he handed me a glass of tea. I drained the cup then he attentively refilled it for me.

Monsieur Gaspard entered the room. He was a tall thin man, dressed in a grey suit and had thinning gray hair.

"Well, this is the Sophia Anderson I have been waiting to meet for many years. Your grandfather was a friend of mine a long time ago. I will let you go if you can give me what I want. Where is the violin I am seeking?" he asked me.

"I don't know. It was not in the vault at Le Mont St. Michel. We were just going to tour France and return home," I hoped he believed me.

"That is the wrong answer. It must be

someplace. I know that your grandfather has hidden it. I know he has given you the means to find it. I am sorry, Miss Anderson, we must detain you."

"Francoise, please come here and bring Maria to help search our guest. Let me know what you find."

After commanding them to search me, he then turned and walked out of the room.

They found nothing on me. Francoise and Maria left and then another man, the one that captured me walked in.

"My name is Thomas, come this way." he said commanding me down the hall.

"You will stay here for now; lunch will be brought to you shortly." he said and walked away.

What am I going to do? Is John outside? Did He follow us? I could have cried, but didn't have time for that, I had to get a hold of myself and figure a way out. I started pacing the room and looking for an escape. I tried the window, but it was locked. Then looked outside and could see the immaculate grounds. *I had to get out of here.*

****

"Park here Kimo. We are just outside the gate and out of site of the house. We need to wait until dark and then I am going in for her." John told Kimo and Susan.

"Ok, said Kimo, "let's watch the neighborhood. I'm happy we were lucky being able to follow her unnoticed to Le Mans.

****

"The time has come," said the messenger when he was seated inside the monastery."

"So, I was afraid of this, I will let the contacts know and they will make the call," the Monsignor told him.

The Monsignor got up and escorted the messenger out. He then walked to the dorm and knocked on a door.

The door opened. "Yes, Monsignor," said the monk.

"It has happened," said the Monsignor.

"I am sorry the time has come, but I will contact the others and we will go within the hour," said the monk.

"Very well, God speed and you are welcome back here when this is over, if you are still alive." The Monsignor then gave him a blessing.

The calls were made and an hour later five men dressed in black robes drove out of the monastery. The car descended down the long windy rode and they arrived at their destination in just a short time.

****

"Ok, it's dark I am going to climb that tree over

to the left," John then got dressed in black and put his wire cutters, night goggles and radio in his pockets.

"John, I will be right there after I dress in black too. Susan stay and be ready to drive us out of here when we get Sophia. Kanani you protect Susan." Kimo said.

"Kimo, actually we might be able to use Kanani. Could you open that closet?" John asked him.
Kimo opened it up.

"If her harness is in there could you grab it?"
Kimo searched the closet.

"It's here John," Kimo replied getting it out and handing it to John.

"Good, I can hoist Kanani up in that and then lift her down the other side. She can find Sophia in the house for us." John told Kimo and Susan.

"I will be ok in here alone, Kimo and John," said Susan. "I will turn off the lights and lock the doors."

"Ok, let's go. I will wait for you outside Kimo," said John. Then he took Kanani and they left the RV.

Kimo showed up and took Kanani. John climbed the tree and put on his night goggles and then he climbed down to talk to Kimo.

"The place is lit up; I don't see any wires above the wall." He then put Kanani's harness on her. "I will hoist her up. Then you need to climb the tree, drop inside the estate. When you're secure, I will lower

Kanani to you. Ok, ready?" John asked Kimo.

"You bet John," said Kimo. "Let's go.

Kimo was inside the estate, Kanani was now on the ground next to him and John descended afterwards.

"Let's sneak up to the house and walk around it, let Kanani sniff for Sophia," said John taking Kanani's lead and telling her what to look for.

****

The car arrived with the men from the Monastery. They parked and scaled the wall, coming into the estate from the back. With them they carried weapons, rope and cameras. They snuck through the kitchen door and entered the house, quietly walking to the wing with the bedrooms. Part of the team went into the gallery and took many photos. One of the men made a call. They were to stay where they were until help arrived. The men inside were to have no contact or fighting with Gaspard or his men if it could be avoided. They sunk into the crevices of the hallway. One man slipped into a bedroom.

****

9

THE DOOR TO THE ROOM I was in creaked open, I held my breath and ducked behind the bed.

"Sophie, it is Grandpa," said Robert Anderson.

"Oh papa, it is you." I said with relief jumping out from behind the bed.

"What's happening? Why are you here? I thought you joined a monastery," I said as I ran over and hugged my beloved grandpa.

"It is a very long story; I have it all written down for you in the vault at the house I left to you. This was a final mission I needed to accomplish. I have been trying to catch this man for most of my career! I must not stay long; I need to go. Here is a card with the real address to come see me. I love you my dear and I say this with a heavy heart. I have missed you and your sister

so much through the years when I had to be away. You will be safe now; I'm happy you married a good, smart man and have such a faithful dog. Stay in this room until someone comes for you. Good bye," grandpa kissed me and got up to leave.

"Papa, don't go please, I have missed you so much and I have so many questions," I pleaded.

"You have my card, come see me after you have gone to the estate. We will arrange a longer visit," he told me. "I must go now."

He then got up and left as quietly as he had entered.

****

He joined the other men in black and quietly left the house without being seen by the guards or officers.

They left the film behind in the agreed place for their contact to pick up and finally put Gaspard out of business for life.

The men drove back up the long driveway to the monastery and entered. Inside the Monsignor and all of the Brothers greeted them.

"This was a job accomplished and well done!" The Monsignor said praising the men. They had a small celebration and then went to the Chapel to pray Vespers and go to sleep.

****

Kimo and John were almost up to the house when they heard sirens; they looked over at the gate.

"Kimo, follow me, hide behind this tree," John told him.

With that the three of them hid, watching the sirens and racing cars speed down the long drive and come to a sudden halt in front of the house.

****

I heard all of the noise and hid under the bed. Two officers from the Department de la Surete-ront broke down the front door and ran in shining flashlights everywhere and shouting.

"Se retirer! We are here to confiscate all of the artwork stolen from private collectors!
Gaspard, give yourself up."

Someone shot at them, so they shot back. A bullet hit a vase and it shattered.

"Stop shooting, you are breaking valuable things!" Gaspard shouted to his men waving his hands in the air. "They have nothing on us." Then he made a dash for the kitchen door.

"You are under arrest, do not resist!" the officer shouted as he chased Gaspard into the kitchen knocking him down and grabbing him.

"I will not be treated like this! You will not get away with it!" Gaspard yelled as he was handcuffed.

Other officers arrested the employees in the house.

"We just work for him, we know nothing,"

"Tell that to the Cour d'Assises!" The officer said leading them away.

****

John told me what they had done to find me and this is how it played out.

As the men were scruffily taken away, John, Kimo and Kanani ran through the broken down door. John held out his retired FBI badge.

"We're here to find my wife who was kidnapped," John told the Officer.

"Where is she and why was she kidnapped?" asked the officer.

"Gaspard wanted a violin my wife has inherited," John told him.

"Men, search the house for a woman! You Monsieur, come with me we will search the rest of the house," ordered the officer.

I was rescued by an officer, which opened the door to the room I was in.

****

"I'm Sophie!" I told him holding up my
hands.

"Good, come with me," the officer said. "Let me
radio the rest of the team and let them know you've
been located."

With that he grabbed his walkie-talkie and said,
"I have found the woman and there is another woman
here also."

"Rachael, is that you?" I asked as I ran into her
in the hallway.

"Yes, can you believe the trouble I have had just
delivering that violin to you! I was just doing a favor
for my family's dear friend, which turned out to be
your grandfather. Then I was kidnapped off the Port
Townsend ferry in Washington State and brought here.
It's been a terrible ordeal and I can't wait to go home,"
Rachael told me.

Both of us were taken to the front of the house.

"John, Kimo, Kanani!" I cried running over to
them.

"Sophie, are you alright," John asked, putting his
arms around me and giving me a big bear hug.

"I think so, oh, here's Rachael, remember I told
you about her," I answered.

"Yes you did. Rachael I'm John, this is Kimo
and Kanani," John said reaching out his hand and
shaking hers.

"Nice meeting you too. Now, do you think these

gentlemen can arrange to get me to Paris tonight?" she asked John as she pointed to the *Sûreté*.

"They want to ask you some questions so why don't you ask them that." he told her.

"Good idea. I'll go talk to them now. Thank you for saving me!" she said.

"You are welcome and we are sorry about this whole mess," I told her.

"I never thought doing a favor for my father's old friend would have gotten me into this predicament with the biggest thief in the World! Take care and Bon Chance," she said as she walked away.

John turned back to me and said, "Let's blow this joint sweetheart!"

"I agree," I put my arm through his and the four of us walked out of the house down the long drive.

Susan was out of the RV in a flash running our way.

"Sophie! You're alright!" she said as she reached us. Then she gave me a big hug twirling me around on my heels.

"Pretty much so, just a bit shaken," I told her hugging her back.

"Let's get back to our hotel at Le Mont St. Michel tonight and have a nice relaxing dinner and evening." John suggested.

"Great idea," I said and the others agreed too.

We climbed in the RV and drove back to our

hotel. At dinner I filled them in on my adventure and told them about my grandpa's surprise visit.

"Wow, that was a shock seeing him, wasn't it Sophie?" asked Susan.

"Yes, he was dressed as a monk and looked very peaceful. He gave me his card, so I can go see him." I pulled out the card and passed it around for everyone to look at.

"That's some story, you know you should write a book Sophie," said Kimo.

"Maybe when we get back home I will," I told all of them.

"Tomorrow we are on our way to Luxembourg! I wonder what we'll find?" I asked Susan.

"I don't know, Sophie. I'm excited too." Susan answered.

"I was in Luxembourg when I was seven years old with my grandparents. We lived in the town square in an apartment. It was the biggest apartment I'd ever seen. I thought other people lived in the rooms next to us, LOL." I told them.

"Why was that, Sophie," asked John.

I continued, "we only used the kitchen with the coal stove and the bedrooms. I had no idea there was a sitting room and formal dining room, until we visited some neighbors and their apartment had all of that. That's when I realized we did too. Funny how things look so different when you're little isn't it?" I asked.

"Yes it is," said Susan. "I remember what it was like growing up on Maui being a white girl, then I met Kimo and all of that changed."

"Oh, Susan you are my sweetie," said Kimo. "No one bothered or teased you again after I met you." He gave her a quick hug.

Just then my cell phone started ringing. It was in my pocket, so I pulled it out. It was Leila, my niece.

"Hi sweetie, it's nice to hear from you. How is your mom and dad and how are you doing?" I asked her.

"Oh, Auntie," she was sobbing into the phone. "I am at the Egyptian Embassy right now."

"What, why are you there what's wrong sweetie?" I asked her.

"Mom and Dad took a job in Egypt at an archeological dig. We had a campsite and they left me a month ago in camp to catch up on some reading while they explored. They never returned, not any of them!" Leila sighed.

"Oh no, that's horrible!" I cried into the phone. "This is awful."

"Sophie what happened?" John wanted to know.

I motioned just a minute to him. "How did you get to the embassy?" I asked her.

"I walked a several kilometers to another dig site. I stayed with them for a few days while they went looking for my parents and their team. After three days they gave up and decided to bring me here," she finished with a sigh.

"You should have called me right away dear. I'm going to wire some money to you and book a flight for you into Luxembourg. I need to speak to someone in the Embassy; can you get anyone to speak to me right now?"

"Yes just a minute," Leila told me and put down the phone to get someone.

I took that opportunity to tell the others what this was about.

"My sister and brother-in-law are missing in Egypt; they were on an archeological dig and did not return one night and that was a month ago! Leila is at the Embassy and we need to pick her up in Luxembourg. Can you try to book a flight for her for Friday, Susan?" I asked my friend.

"Yes, let's go to the room and do all of this," Susan answered getting up from the table. She had her dark hair tied into a ponytail; she was wearing stretch pants and a designer blouse that looked great on her rather thin medium height frame.

I looked down at my attire; I was still in my long black skirt and jean jacket with my leather cowboy boots on. I needed to change and get cleaned up. We got up and went into our room.

"Aunt Sophie, here is a lady to help me," Leila said handing the phone over.

"Hi, I am Mrs. Sandover, what can I do to help your niece?" she asked me.

"Well, I want to wire her some money so she has some cash. Then I will have to get back to you with airline reservations. I will pick her up at the Luxembourg airport on Friday. This is Monday, I'm in France and it will take me a couple of days to get there." I finished by saying, "Where do I wire the money and how do I contact you?"

She gave me her contact information and the Embassy bank's wiring address. They were going to feed and keep her all week. I told them I would reimburse them.

"Ok, Sophie, I have her booked on a flight leaving Thursday night at six p.m. from Cairo, arriving in Luxembourg Friday at noon."

"Great, Susan, thank you," I told her.

"Mrs. Sandover, we have her flight number right now. Let me give you the information." I gave it to her over the phone.

"Thank you Sophia," said Mrs. Sandover. "I will make sure she is taken care of all week and get her on that flight."

"Thank you so much, do you have any news on my sister and brother-in-law?" I asked.

"No, these digs are very dangerous right now. There are bandits and thieves. They watch until the archeologists find something and rob them, sometimes taking them or killing them right there. We warn people not to go before they set out to do this, but most of them don't listen." she finished telling me.

"Is there any chance I can come over and search for them?" I asked her.

"It would be at your own risk and you probably would not find them. We highly discourage it," she said.

"Ok, may I speak with Leila please?" I asked her.

"Yes, she is right here. Goodbye, please call if you need to, and you have my number." Mrs. Sandover said.

"Thank you again." I told her before she handed the phone over to Leila.

"Leila, we are picking you up in Luxembourg on Friday." I told my niece.

"I heard, thank you so much, but I thought you were in Port Townsend. I have missed you and this has been very terrifying for me." she told me.

"I know sweetie, please call me every day until you leave. We are in France right now; it's a long story, I will tell you all about when I have you in my arms again, I can't wait! I am going to reimburse the Embassy for all of the phone calls. Try to hang in there, you are very brave." I reassured her.

"Bye and thank you Auntie," Leila said with a sigh.

"Bye sweetie, I love you more than rice and beans," I told her and then I got a laugh out of her.

"Ok, pumpkin, I will talk to you tomorrow, call me in the evening," I told her.

"Ok, bye," she said, and then hung up.

"Boy, that's a tough one," I said getting off the phone. "I wonder where my sister is?" I asked looking at my husband and friends.

"I don't know honey, first let's get Leila and then see what we can do," John told me.

"Ok, I know you're right. When can we get our other RV from the French police?" I asked John.

"They have my number and will call me when it can be released."

"Great, well is anyone tired or do you want to play cards?" I asked my friends.

"We are beat and so are you. We'll see you in the morning for breakfast," Kimo said giving me a hug goodnight.

"Ok, see you guys in the morning," I said. After everyone hugged, they left us for the night.

I tossed and turned all night dreaming about my sister.

****

I was young living in Luxembourg with my grandparents and sister. One day when we were out playing, my older sister dared me to climb in with a bull grazing in a pasture and grab some apples off a tree. I was feeling very brave. If the farmer caught us, we would be in trouble. I climbed over the railed fence to the other side, slowly climbed down. I was watching the bull; he had not seen me yet. I held on to the fence until I got to the tree, then he saw me! The bull charged at me, I froze for at least a minute. It felt like longer.

Jennie let out a blood-curdling scream!

10

I CLIMBED THE TREE and yelled for her to distract the bull, so I could get out of the pasture. She ran down to the other end of the pasture and the bull ran beside her.

"Sophie, run for your life!"

I scurried down from the tree and over the fence. I was shaking so badly I had to sit down. She came back over and hugged me.

"I'm sorry for daring you to do that Sophie, don't tell Grandma or Grandpa." she chided me.

"No way would I do that, but I almost got killed!" I said standing up and shaking dirt off my shorts. I glared at her and stamped off towards home. Jennie followed me.

****

I sat up in bed sweating. Kanani came over and kissed me.

Sophie you had a nightmare. I'm here we are ok.

I hugged Kanani and laid back down. I tried to rest until the sun came up. Where could Jennie be and what happened to her? I thought my heart was going to break.

The next morning, we all met for breakfast. I was showered, dressed and drinking coffee when John, Kimo and Susan sat down next to me.

"What's wrong Sophie?" John asked me, you look like you didn't sleep last night.

"I didn't sleep well, I kept dreaming about Jennie," I told him.

"I am sorry honey, let's focus on Leila's arrival and getting to the estate so we can finally see the violin. Then we can decide what to do about Jennie and Robert," John told me taking my chin in his hand and giving me an affectionate kiss. "Let's eat and get started on our journey."

"Ok," I told him with a sigh. With that we ordered our breakfast and walked through the village one more time. Susan bought some souvenirs and then we loaded the RV and drove off through the lovely French countryside. That night we checked into an RV park just outside Reims and had our last French dinner of salad, fish, Bordeaux wine and fish.

Looking at the map the next morning, I showed Susan what I was looking at.

"We could actually go to the house in Luxembourg, spend the night and see the violin before picking up Leila if we took this route." I pointed to the autobahn that left Mont St. Michel and took us though the town of Nancy, leading us straight across the border in Luxembourg.

"Let's see if the guys think it's a good idea," I told Susan as I got out of my seat and showed John and Kimo the map.

"Looks like a plan," John agreed after looking at what I showed him. Kimo seconded the motion after looking at it too.

"Great, I can't wait to get there," I said retaking my seat and planning out the route.

We got to Luxembourg by midday. We drove into the city center of Echternach.

"Look," I said pointing, "that is where I lived when I was seven years old before Grandpa bought the house we're going to now! Around the corner from here there used to be a pastry shop. That is about all I remember."

"Amazing, it must feel strange being back here Sophie," said Susan.

"It is a strange feeling, but I like it," I added. We stopped and asked directions to Rue de la Blanc. It took us about five minutes to locate the road.

"Look, it should be that house up there on the right, the addresses are getting closer." I was saying leaning over John while the poor guy was trying to drive.

"Yes, I think that is the address, Sophie," said John.

He pulled up to the gate.

"Wow, look at this place!" Kimo was so excited.

"I know," I said, running out of the RV with Kanani in hot pursuit.

Susan jumped out too.

"I put in the code Grandpa wrote on his business card. Good thing I saw him that night or we could not have gotten through the gate without taking it down."

"Really!" said Susan.

"Ok," I motioned for John to drive through as the electric gate opened for him. Susan, Kanani and I ran through too, before it closed.

"Look at the grounds Susan, Kanani run girl!" I told her as we started jogging with her following the RV.

This is so fun! Look a squirrel I can chase. He he, I love it here. I'm going to race back to Sophie now!

There were beautiful manicured gardens and the entire property was fenced, lined with tall trees. It made the five acres very private. It was also relatively flat. The house was a mile from the gate so the guys were waiting for us on the doorstep by the time we got there.

Opening the door, I was so excited I fumbled with the key; we walked into a large foyer with tall ceilings. The kitchen was at the rear of the house. There was a library to our left and a long hallway with bedrooms to the right. It was one story with marble floors and a beautiful chandelier hanging over our heads in the entry.

"I have never seen a prettier house in my life," said Kimo in awe.

"I know what you mean," Susan said with her mouth wide open as she looked around.

I chimed in, "I did not even hope to dream of something so wonderful and grand. It's too wonderful!"

We ran into the kitchen, "look at that deck, and look at this kitchen. It's beautiful, just right for a chef. This will be fun to cook in won't it Susan?" I asked her.

"Oh, yes it will, Sophie," she said.

"Hey, don't leave me out," said John grinning. "I cook pretty well."

"Yes you do, honey," I told him.

"Girls, why don't you go find a market, grab some steaks, salad, and wine. We will unload the RV first, so you can take it shopping and then we will put things away while you're gone," John stated.

"Great idea, come on Susan let's help them unload the RV and then we can go shopping," I told her walking out the front door.

"I am right behind you my friend," Susan said.

The RV was unloaded and we took off to find a market. We found a grand market!

"Wow, I better not buy too much. Leila would love to come here and help us load up on food when she gets here." I told Susan.

"I know, it's hard not to load up on the good stuff in here," Susan said.

" I am in love with this country," I told her.

"Me too, I can't wait to see how the guys feel," Susan added.

"I have a filling we might be moving here," I told her giggling.

"Let's hope so, this is the best place we have been yet," Susan said.

I agreed and we went through the checkout line and headed home.

The guys unloaded the groceries and cooked dinner. Susan and I walked through the bedrooms and picked out which ones we wanted.
After finishing a great dinner, sitting on the deck I looked at John.

"We have not seen the violin," I said smacking my forehead standing up. I was taken in by the majesty of the estate and had completely forgotten about the violin.

"Good grief, you're right Sophie," stated John. He got up and grabbed the plates, Kimo, Susan, and I grabbed the rest and we put everything in the sink to be washed later.

We found the safe in the library. I put in the key and opened it up. I switched on the light and we looked for the most magnificent violin that had ever been seen by any of us in our lifetime. It was gone!

11

MY HEART SANK to my toes.

"Sophie, a note," said John running over to a note pinned on a board.

"What does it say?" I ran over looking at it.

"I'll read it out loud," said John.

Madam Sophia,

Sorry to disappoint you, but your sister is on to something. I want it bad enough to make you find her, so I can have it too. She has disappeared, so I think she found what she was looking for. I will be watching to see if you find her secret. The violin will be safe as long as you search for your sister with all earnest intent. If you do not find what I

want or make an effort, I will smash it! It means nothing to me. I am serious about this and nothing will stop me getting what I want so desperately.

Sincerely,

Roberto Barras

"Well, the nerve!" I cried, "what does my sister

have to do with this? How does he know she is missing? How did he know about the violin? How did he get in here?"

"I don't have any answers, honey. We will get to the meaning of this somehow though," John told me while he looked at me with determination.

"Oh Sophie," cried Susan running over to look at the note. "This is not happening, surely it is not! This must be so unsettling for you!"

"We might be able to find something out from Leila when we get her," Kimo tried reassuring me.

"I am sure you're right," Kimo I replied.
I could not listen to what anyone was saying. I was devastated and disappointed beyond belief! Just to add more to my grief, my sister was missing too. Looking around I saw boxes and boxes. "Look, I bet those are Grandpa's stories about his life," I said pointing.

"I bet they are," said John bending over and lifting off the lid from one box.

"Ah look here, it's the start of your grandfather's story. This will take a long time to go through, but it will be so much fun and interesting for you Sophie," John said; giving me a little smile to perk me up.

"I know John," I said taking a paper out of the box and looking at it. Finally, I put it back and John placed the lid on the box.

"This is for another time, let's go clean up," I told Susan.

"I agree," she said.

"You guys go back and sit down outside, you cooked dinner. We'll join you after we clean up the mess," I told them.

"Are you sure, sweetie," John asked giving me a kiss on the check.

"Yes I am," I said as we walked out of the safe, locking it behind us. We finished our evening with heavy hearts, even though we were happy to be in the house. Tomorrow was Thursday; we decided to leave early the next day so we could be at the airport with plenty of time before Leila arrived. I had to find my sister and Leila was the key.

12

ANXIOUSLY AWAITING Leila to disembark from her plane, I was pacing like crazy in the Luxembourg Airport. Finally, John got my attention and told me the plane was unloading. I stopped pacing and looked up. Yes, they were unloading the passengers now.

"Leila!" I called as I ran over to her. She was dressed in khaki Capri's, a khaki t-shirt with Egyptian writing on it, black tennis shoes, and a black backpack with all of her belongings.

"Auntie Sophie," Leila cried running into my arms.

"It's so nice to see you again; you look ok for what you have been through. Come on, Leila. John, Susan and Kimo are here too," I put my arm around her and walked her over to them.

Everyone got their hellos and hugs in, even Kanani.

Alright Leila's back, we always have fun together, I'm so happy. Kanani was thumping her tail.

"Let's get in the RV and head home, Leila," I told her.

"Sounds good to me," she answered.

With that we all got back into our RV and drove

home.

While we were driving I was being patient, but really wanted to know what happened.

"Leila, what is going on, what happened?" I asked her with a great deal of concern in my voice.

"It's a long story," Leila lowered her head.

"Well, I need to hear it. I need to find your mom and dad," I told her.

Raising her sweet face, she brushed her bangs out of her eyes, slipping her backpack off, and removed her shoes. She was getting comfortable.

"Mom and Dad were in Egypt chasing a rumor. All of the archaeologists were looking for this and working together." she continued, "there was supposed to be a door or entryway that leads to some other times. I think it's called time traveling. They were searching for it, but not finding it. Then the last morning I ever saw them, they were going to a different location. They left me at the camp with Rufi, he is an Egyptian boy about twelve years old. His dad was working with my parents. They wanted us to stay in case they really found something, so we would be safe. We were told not to leave the camp, but wait there for them. They were sure they would not find anything and be back by dark. We waited until the next morning. No sign of them. We waited until that evening, still nothing. So the next morning we walked to the camp nearest us for help. Rufi's Uncle Steve was in that camp and we knew he would help us. It took all day to walk there. When we got there we told them what happened. They were very concerned. The next day Uncle Steve took some men and drove us back we to our camp. We stayed there three weeks while the men looked for our parents and the secret door. Finding nothing after that amount of time, they took me to the U.S. Embassy.

No one in the Embassy knows about this at all, they think robbers have been killing or kidnapping the archeologists." Leila finished her story and sighed.

"Wow, that is some story," I said getting up to get her a glass of water.

"Thank you," she said taking a big gulp and putting the glass down.

"This secret door is supposed to lead to another time period?" I asked her.

"No one knows, but it is supposed to be the best place on earth or something like that," she said making a funny face.

"Well, that is a story in itself. If that were true then that is why my violin is being held ransom," I said looking at Susan.

"Most likely, Sophie," Susan answered.

"What about a violin?" Leila wanted to know.

"Grandpa left me a violin, he left me his house. Your mom has money put away for her in a bank from him. You will always be taken care of,

Leila. I really want to find my sister, now that I know she is more than likely still alive and not kidnapped." I told her and Susan both.

"What happened to great grandpa, is he dead?" Leila jumped up crying out.

"No Leila, he joined a Catholic order of monks, I am sorry for not telling you!" I told her giving her a quick hug.

"Wow that is really neat. Can we go see him sometime?" she asked me changing her sorrow into joy.

"Yes, we can and will do that soon," I assured her.

"Should we tell the guys?" Susan asked me after Leila had settled down.

"Let's wait until we get home and see what happens." I told her.

"Good plan," Susan agreed.

"Great, so we are going to Echternach?" Leila's eyes got big.

"Yes, we have not discussed it with the guys, but I think we might just stay there," I told her.

"It sounds like an adventure," Leila's eyes lit up a bit.

"Let me go talk to John and Kimo." I turned to Susan, "Susan do you think you and Kimo would like to live in Luxembourg and just use Port Townsend when we want?" I asked her.

"Yes, I am so glad you asked, I've been thinking the same thing!" Susan exclaimed jumping up and hugging Leila, then me.

"Ok," I laughed, "I'll ask the guys." I wondered over to John.

"Hi Honey," said John.

"Hi," I answered.

"How is Leila? Did you find out anything?" He asked me.

"She will be ok and we will tell you her story later. I have a question?"

"Ok, what is it?" he said.

"How about if we stay in Luxembourg?"

"I would like that Sophie, how do you feel about it Kimo?" John asked him.

"Susan and I would like to stay; we have already talked about it." he said.

"Ok, then we need to go back to Port Townsend and get some things out of our houses," John told Kimo.

Then looking at me he said, "do you want to sell your shop or lease it?"

John waited for me to answer. I told him that I had a friend that wanted to buy the shop. If he could contact her and take care of that for me, I would be grateful. It was a helpful idea for them to go back and do this.

"Yes, we can do that. How about the first of next

week?" John asked Kimo.

"It depends on how the girls feel about us going that soon," Kimo answered.

"Yes, it sounds like a great plan," I assured them. I had a motive of course. "Then Susan and I can get Leila settled. We will all be in a new place and it will be good for her. Let me give the girls the news," I said giving him a kiss on his check and standing up stretching.

I walked to the back and gave Susan and Leila the news. John and Kimo could hear cheering in the back of the RV.

We pulled into our place quite late at night. Leila was sleepy, so I walked her into the house and put her into a bedroom tucking her in.

"Thank you Aunt Sophie for loving me so much. I just know my mom and dad found that secret door. Can we go find it too?" she asked looking at me with the cutest expression.

"Let me talk it over with Uncle John and Uncle Kimo, we'll make a decision tomorrow." I told her as I gave her a kiss goodnight. "Try to sleep now and I will see you in the morning and give you a tour of the house and town."

"Ok, goodnight," Leila turned over on her side and closed her eyes.

I left the room quietly and walked into the kitchen. Everyone was sitting around the table drinking tea and talking. I pulled up a chair and joined the conversation.

"You wanted to know her story," I told John. "I will tell it the best I can." I then told them the story Leila told Susan and me. Finishing I asked, "What do you guys think?"

"It sounds like a crazy idea, but the guy that stole your violin believes it. So do the other archeologists searching for the same thing. I think maybe someone found something, came back and told his tale or it's all a fable," John stated.

"It's pretty farfetched," said Kimo shaking his head. "However we need to at least look for your sister and her husband, Sophie."

"Well I feel the same way," I told them. Susan shook her head in agreement.

"Do you think that you guys can go to Port Townsend and take care of business next week, and then Susan, Leila, and I will make a trip to Egypt and see what we can dig up? No pun intended." Sophie said trying to inject a little humor into the conversation.

"What about Kanani?" John and Kimo both asked me.

"Well, she comes with me of course."

Of course I do! Really! You think Sophie would leave me John?

"Ok, as long as you are very careful and keep in

touch with us. I will give you one week. Then we will meet back here and talk about what you found." John finished and then said, "let's go to sleep."

"Great idea on both accounts," I added and stood up.

We all said good night and decided to tour Luxembourg with Leila tomorrow and have a relaxing day.

I woke up to a beautiful Saturday morning. Turning over to wake up John, I discovered he was already up. Kanani was still sleeping on my legs. I told her good morning, wiggled free, and I jumped out of bed. She followed me into the shower, and then I dressed in Capri's, tennis shoes, and a stretch top. I tied up my wet hair into a French braid and put on a little makeup. Walking out into the kitchen I smelled bacon and coffee.

"Ummm, smells good," I said walking over and greeting John.

"Good morning sleepy head, you smell fresh," he told me. He put down the coffee pot after pouring me a cup and gave me a kiss on the cheek.

"Thank you for this," I said taking a sip. "Is everyone else still asleep?"

"No, Leila is outside walking around the grounds; Susan and Kimo went into town and bought this food for breakfast. They are taking a shower now and getting cleaned up. They will be right out. Why don't you go find Leila and have her come in?" John asked me.

"Great idea," I took my coffee cup and walked outside. Kanani ran out and relieved herself then ran over to Leila and dropped a ball in front of her.

Morning Leila let's play catch!

She threw it for Kanani. Kanani chased it and brought it back to be thrown again.

"Good morning Aunt Sophie," called Leila.

"Good morning Leila, come in for breakfast with Kanani," I told her.

"Ok," she said, grabbing Kanani's ball and running over to me.

Oh, that was so fun. Oh well, I like to eat just as well as I like chasing my ball. Kanani ran ahead and waited for me by the back door to let her in.

"Did you sleep well?" I asked her when she got there, giving Kanani a scratch on the head.

"Yes, I did. It's nice to be in a house feeling loved and secure with clean sheets and a hot shower. Can I stay with you forever, even after we find Mom and Dad?" she asked me hopefully.

"Let's find them and see what happens, but you will always be welcome to live here with us." I told her.

She seemed satisfied with the answer, so we walked inside. After breakfast we jumped into the RV and went to a dealership to buy a car. We ended up buying two BMW's. We left the RV and one BMW at the lot then took off to tour Luxembourg. We picked up the car and RV on the way home to the estate. Monday morning came too soon, but we had things to do. John and Kimo took off for Port Townsend, WA. Kanani, Susan, Leila and I caught a flight to Egypt.

We stayed in a hotel that first night; I kept looking to see that no one was watching us. The next morning, we rented a jeep and drove out to the camp where Leila's friend, Rufi, was with his Uncle. After introductions they offered us to stay with them and they would help us look for the secret door that allows time travel.

Sitting around the fire Rufi's Uncle Richard began the story.

"This is not a fairy tale, someone found this other world and came back to tell others. Then he mysteriously disappeared without reviling where the opening is. There is supposedly a door that you can enter, then a door that comes back to this world, but they are not together. We have found a door, but cannot open it. We will show you tomorrow, but I believe it is a one-way door to come back to our world. I believe the others have found the entry door, but not the exit door, or they don't want to come back. However, I know my brother would come back for his son, just as Leila's parents would come back for her if they could," he finished saying looking at Leila.

"Of course, I could just be blowing smoke, I don't know anything for certain."

She was shaking her head in agreement.

"Wow that is some tale. I am anxious to get started; I need to tell you that there is a man named Roberto Barras that has stolen something from me of great value. He will not return it until I show him how my sister disappeared. Have you heard of this man?" I asked him.

"Roberto Barras, that rat!" Uncle Steve said, throwing a stick into the fire. "He has been bothering all of us for years! He can have the new world and stay there for all I care. Let's hope we find it tomorrow." He finished then and stood up, "Why don't we retire and get an early start?"

We agreed with him and all of us girls slept in a big tent together. Morning came quickly and after breakfast we got into our jeep following Steve and his men. They stopped after about half an hour and we all got out. We were on a plain, and it was very hot. In front of us was a steep slope and beyond that were rock walls; I couldn't see any openings from the jeep. We were the only people here and it was a bit eerie.

"There, you can see an outline in the wall," Steve said pointing.

"I see something now that you've pointed it out," I said. "Can we try to open it?"

"Yes, let's go," he said leading us down a steep

embankment.

Reaching the wall, I touched the door pushing on it.

"It doesn't budge, does it?" I asked Steve.

"No, we have marked the location though. If you were on the other side maybe it opens. I don't know how you would find it on the other side, because I have never been there. It's pretty risky business," he said.

We finished and jumped back into the jeeps driving back to camp. Then Leila and Rufi led all of us off in the direction of where their parents ventured that fateful morning. All of us spread out. Leila, Susan, Kanani, Rufi and I went one way and the rest went the other way.

At noon we sat down and had a bit of lunch under some shade. It was pretty hot out.

"Look over there," I said pointing.

"Wow, it looks like a crack in the wall," said Susan.

We all got up and ran over to the shape. I placed my hands on one side of the crack and pushed, nothing moved. So I tried the other side, it opened up!

"Rufi and Leila, hurry go get Steve and his men!" I told them.

"Susan, please help me push this open all the way?" I asked her. She walked over and helped me push it open.

"Wait Sophie, don't go in!" she said.

I was shoved from behind away from the door and a violin case was thrown at me. Susan caught it screaming at the man who shoved me. He ran through the door and disappeared! Kanani chased him in!

You rat, I'm going to get you for hurting my Sophie.

13

"WHAT HAPPENED?" I asked Susan picking myself up dusting off my clothes. I turned looking around for Kanani but didn't see her anywhere.

"I think we just met Roberto Barras. He ran through that door before tossing this violin to me. Kanani chased him Sophie!" Susan screamed while handing me the violin case she was holding.

"Good grief, we need to open that door again and get her back." I said taking it from her and setting it down against the wall. I am going in there." I said with determination.

"Ok, Sophie, I will look after it, but don't go in too far."

"Ok, I promise," I said.

The door was opened and Susan was leaning on it. I walked through; there was a long tunnel. I turned on my flashlight and walked about a 100 yards, and then I saw several portals. I stepped through the first one, I turned and looked back towards Susan, but I couldn't see her or anything of where I was. I just entered a new world separate from the one I was just in. I called to Susan, but she either couldn't hear me or my voice couldn't penetrate through the portal. I was now on my own. First I needed to find Kanani, I just hoped Susan was holding that door open.

"Kanani," I called. I could hear her barking. "Kanani come!"

Woof woof, *I'm coming back Sophie, wait for me. I didn't get the bad guy though.*

Thank goodness she listened to my voice and came back. She was jumping all over me, wagging her tail trying to make me go with her.

I love you Sophie, I was so scared when you weren't behind me. But I'm here now so we're ok, right?

"We need to get out of here. Look Kanani, what's this?" I asked her bending over and picking up the notes.

"Ok, we need to go girl." I said hugging her then grabbing her collar and walking back through the portal and into the tunnel. I was walking on the other side of the tunnel now hugging the wall with my right hand. We weren't through time in the tunnel, I was sure of it.

I looked up and could see Susan in the distance still holding the door open.

"Susan can you hear me?" I shouted.

"Yes, thank goodness your coming back! Is that Kanani with you?" Susan asked with relief in her voice.

"Yes, I have her and I found something when I went through the portal looking for Kanani. Don't let go of the door and we'll be right there." I shouted back to her.

"What did you find?" she asked me.

"Notes," I told her. "I think I have all of them. I'm bringing them out." Then Kanani and I walked out of the tunnel through the door.

Putting them down on the ground, Susan let the door close and joined me.

"They say," I read them aloud placing the pages in order.

"This is Jennie. We found the new world. It is more than we ever imagined. We made the mistake of rushing through the time portal without noticing where we entered and quickly became confused and lost in this new world. We're looking for a way out to get our daughter, Leila. Please, if you read this let her know we are ok. We will find her someday."

"Can you believe this Susan? We found it!" I screamed, jumping up and down.

"Sophie, this is unreal, wait until Leila hears this! Susan exclaimed.

"I know!"

"What did you find?" asked Uncle Steve as he was running up to us with Leila, Rufi, and the other men.

"We found the door that lets you go in. You were right about the entry and exit. Also, here are notes from my sister!" I showed him the notes lined up lying on the ground.

"Leila, your parents are ok. They can't find their way out!" I told her. I showed her the notes and read them to her.

"I knew it all along," said Leila happily. "I knew they were OK. Let's go after them and bring them back."

"Not just yet," I advised. "We need to plan this out so everyone can safely return. Don't forget, Barras is also in there." I reminded her.

After reading the notes aloud the men cheered. I then told them about meeting Roberto Barras and how he tossed the violin at me. I walked over and picked up the violin case laying it down in front of them. I opened it up and everyone came over to look.

"It's the violin I have been looking for!" I told them with happiness.

"It's beautiful," said Susan and the others.

"Well that scoundrel cannot dampen our happiness!" Uncle Steve exclaimed.

"What will you do now?" I asked him.

"We are marking the location of this time portal. We will pack up what we need and go through this door in a few days time." he told me.

"Why a few days?" Leila and Sophie questioned in unison.

"Can't you go in tomorrow?" I was obviously anxious for them to get going before Jennie had a run-in with Barras. Uncle Steve explained they needed time to gather equipment and plan for any contingency.

"Wow, I would love to go too, but we have to go home to our family." I said with some apprehension.

"Aunt Sophie, should I go with them or stay with you?" Leila asked me.

14

"YOU NEED TO STAY "with me," I told her.

"I think so too," she reluctantly agreed. I knew she was tormented knowing she wanted might to see her parents again, but I could not let her stay. I needed to go home talk to John and Grandpa about going back in and finding her.

We shook hands and exchanged information, then got into the jeep and drove back to Cairo spending one more night in a hotel. We flew home to Luxembourg the next morning.
Walking into our house we found the guys were back and unpacking boxes.

"Hi, honey, you beat us home. I have some huge news to tell you!" I said, "but you should go first, my story will be much longer.

"Hi sweetheart, I can't wait to hear what you have to say. So I'll make this quick. I sold your antique shop and got what I thought you wanted out of the house," said John.

"Wow, that's fantastic, thank you!" I said going over and hugging him." I said to them.

"Let's sit down over here. You have your violin! You must have found the secret!" John said with

gationJMMADAMS

excitement.

"Yes, we did and Robero Barras threw the violin at me before he disappeared through the portal. It' must be where my sister is."

"That's an amazing tale, Sophie, we need to let your grandpa know what you found, we can go see him tomorrow." said John.

"Yes, a visit to Grandpa tomorrow for sure." I said.

"Now can you play something on your violin for us?" asked John.

"I thought you'd never ask." I picked up the Stradivarius and started playing. The music from the violin melted everyone's hearts.

Then I asked, "Do you think we should make a journey through that door too?"

"No!" said Kimo, John, and Susan at the same time. Kanani thumped her tail.

I'll go anywhere with you Sophie, I love you.
I just laughed knowing that we would have to go sooner than later.

THE END

125

Read on to get a taste of another exciting adventure by J.M.M. ADAMS

The Mystery of St. Moritz
A Casey Lane and Jackie Lee GSD Mystery

1

"JACKIE LEE, COME here boy, let me take your scarf off."

Casey reached down and untied my scarf, and then she took her water bottle and doused it with water. After that she tied it over my nose and behind my head. It made the breathing a bit easier. She then did the same for herself.

It was pitch black, the building we were in was on fire, the door was jarred or something because we couldn't get out.

There was a sound!

"Casey, Jackie Lee!!! Are you in there? Can you answer if you are?"

Casey looked at me, "It's Peter and T.J., and they found us!"

"Peter, here we are!!!!" Casey yelled, then she grabbed my harness and we stumbled towards his voice.

Peter was hammering the wall; he finally broke a hole in it, and then tore the wood away. He stepped in with T.J. in front and shined a flashlight on us.

"Are you ok?" He asked Casey as she stumbled into his arms.

"Thank you for coming after us, please get us out of here."

"No problem, I'm glad we got here in time to save you." Peter said.

The flames were engulfing the building as he pulled Casey out, I followed T.J.

Hey buddy, that's twice in two years I owe you for saving our lives. I barked.

No trouble, we need to work together now more than ever. I followed your trail and led Peter to you. T.J. barked.

"Ok pups, stop barking until we get safely out of here, let's hurry." Peter had turned back to tell us to be quiet.

We ran down the hill away from the fire and piled into the Jeep, Captain was guarding the vehicle, and we were in danger!

In the Jeep as Pete drove us away, he looked at Casey, "The door was padlocked from the outside, you've gotten too close to the killer; we can't go home, a friend lent us her chalet to hide in."

The road got narrow and we were climbing the mountain.

"We're close to whoever is killing the horses competing in the 'Gubelin Grand Prix of St. Moritz.' The prize money is 135,135 Swiss francs, which comes to something like $138,500 dollars, plus fame and recognition. All I can say is thank goodness for T.J. being so good at scent and finding us." Casey replied.

"Casey, T.J., Captain and I want to join you and Jackie Lee, the GSD Agency, and be a part of your team. I don't need the money and you know I don't need to work. You wouldn't either if you'd marry me." Peter was concentrating on the road.

I think he was serious but of course Casey didn't jump with an answer.

Casey looked at him, "Why Peter, that's a funny way of asking me."

"Well, you're so busy I haven't had time to make it romantic, but I can tonight." He grinned at her.

"Let's get to the place and get cleaned up, all I can smell is smoke."

Peter told her, "That place is toast behind us; they meant to kill you and Jackie Lee! I'm not going to let that happen on my watch."

Casey squeezed his arm; "You and T.J. are definitely our hero's."

Then Peter, keeping his hands on the steering wheel and navigating the windy, muddy and curvy road up to the chalet said, "Casey, the first time I saw you on Sandy Island and I looked at you, then met you, my heart melted and I fell in love with you. You have brought fun, happiness, adventure and life back into my life and T.J.'s too. You melt my heart and you're the smartest, kindest person I could ever want to know. The way you look at Jackie Lee and all of our dogs I see the person you really are. It makes me love you even more. These last couple of months here in Switzerland with you have made me look at myself even more. I will make it special when I ask you."

Well it's about time, I barked to T.J.

Woof! T.J. answered.

Casey looked at us and laughed.

"Peter, that is the kindest thing anyone ever said to me, except for Steve right before Jackie Lee and I were thrown out of the airplane in that horrible storm. So, hold on to that thought because I think there's trouble ahead!" Casey grabbed the dashboard.

"No kidding, what are all of the police doing?" Peter pulled the Jeep over to the side of the road and rolled down his window.

The policeman approached, "Sir, you can't pass this way, there's a hostage situation."

He pointed down the road, "If you go back about a mile, there's an access road to the chalets up the hill. Take a left and follow the road up, you will miss this mess."

"Thank you, sir." Peter rolled up the window and started backing down the hill.

The wind was howling and dusk was falling, the trees threw a shadow over the road, Peter took it slow, it seemed like forever, but we finely made it up to our chalet. Peter pulled in the driveway and let us out. We got inside the chalet, it was an A Frame; and I couldn't see much because it was too dark. Peter flipped the light switch.

"No power Casey, I have a flashlight in the Jeep let me go get it for you and I'll get the fire going. It's nice they have wood stacked on the porch." Peter came back and handed the flashlight to Casey.

"Thank you Peter, let me hold the flashlight for you until you get the fire going."

"Thank you Casey, let's find some lanterns after I light the fire."

The fire was lit; there were lanterns in every room. Peter lit them, it was pretty cozy, then Peter took us dogs into the kitchen and fed us while Casey showered and changed. She joined us all refreshed, Peter set out crackers, cheese, salami and wine on a table in the living room. He and Casey sat on the big cozy chair by the fire, I stuck close to Casey, Captain was over by the fire and T.J. was in between Casey and Peter's legs on the throw rug.

"Casey, you and Jackie Lee could have been killed if we hadn't arrived in time. Please tell me how the two of you got trapped in that building." Peter took a sip of his wine, there was still no power.

"There was a letter addressed to me under our front doormat this morning. You were already gone, I opened it and it said that someone had information to the whereabouts of the killer. I left Captain to watch the villa, T.J. was off with you, so I left that note you found from me with the address we were going to and Jackie Lee and I took off. We got to the meeting place, it was an old warehouse, the door was opened and the light was on. I stopped at the door, said hello and we stepped inside. As soon as we did the door slammed, I turned to push it back open and couldn't budge it, and then the lights went out. I was really frightened; I held on to Jackie Lee and walked along the wall looking for a way out. That's when we smelled smoke! I covered our faces with the handkerchiefs after soaking them in my drinking water. That's when you saved the day making a hole in that wall to get us out! I've never been so frightened in my life!" Casey grabbed Peter's hand, "we need to narrow this down."

"Casey, they know where we live, that's why we are staying here; in the morning we'll go back to our villa and get a list of all of the neighbors. Someone knows something. I'm ready to pull you out of this mystery, it's gotten too dangerous."

"Peter, we need to solve it, no more horses need to die or disappear!" Casey sounded determined not to quit.

Everything went smoothly that night, to my relief no big events happened. The next morning all of us piled into Baron's truck. We headed back to the place we went yesterday. Baron stopped at all of the local places and asked if anyone had seen new people, anything strange lately, his horse. He showed her picture all around. Then we unhitched the horse trailer and took the truck up the road to the house. We looked through the windows of the house, no one was there, the barn was the same. Then I saw something we hadn't noticed yesterday!

"Five top contender horses have been eliminated by either disappearing or poisoning. The big event takes place in four weeks. We need to figure out if it's another contender doing this or someone else. We've visited with the owners, we've covered all of the questions, like is it a disgruntled jockey or trainer. No one has admitted anything. We're meeting Andre in the morning at our villa; he's the retired police chief that I introduced you to when we first arrived. The police department has brought him back in to help on the case. I went to the police station this morning for a meeting, I'm now a deputy." He reached in his pocket and took out a badge, "I don't want you or Jackie Lee to go anywhere without me knowing until this case is solved."

"That's impressive," Casey took it and checked it over, then handed it back. "Any suggestions?"

"Andre has some, we'll find out in the morning, we might as well get to sleep early, there's no electricity anyway." Peter got up and took Casey's hand, "Come on, I'll put you and Jackie Lee in your room. I'm sleeping out here with Captain and T.J."

"Just let me take a lantern and I'll find my way." Casey hugged him, "Good night."

"Good night Casey and Jackie Lee." Peter rubbed my head, "Look after our girl tonight kiddo."

I wagged my tail and followed Casey into a dark bedroom; I jumped on the bed and waited for her, not a bad mattress. Before I knew it I was sound asleep.

Casey had her arm resting over my shoulder and I felt secure, I might have been snoring. Casey usually pokes me if I snore, but after the day we just completed another surprise would be too much.

Then it happened!

Our window shattered!

2

"JACKIE LEE!" CASEY shot out of bed and looked at me in the dark, "what happened?"

Before I could answer, Peter came busting in through the door, shining his flashlight all around the room.

"Stay there Casey, in fact, get back on the bed and get off on this side, you too Jackie Lee. The window is shattered and glass is everywhere!"

"What happened?" Casey asked Peter.

"I'm not sure how this happened; we'll have to wait until morning. I'll call Andre first thing and let him know about this. Come with me, all of us can sleep by the fireplace in the living room." Peter took Casey's hand and I followed.

I found a cozy rug and snuggled up in it, soon asleep. I was just too tired to stay awake and to listen to Casey and Peter's conversation.

The next morning power was back on, Peter went outside and looked at the window from the outside, I went with him, T.J. came along and so did Captain. Peter saw footprints under the window, so he kept us back. He took out his phone and called Andre. He told him what had happened, then hung up.

"Let's go tell Casey, the police are coming out to get footprints and see what they can come up with." Peter hurried back around the house.

"Andre's coming sweetie, let's look in the phone book for a window repair person." Peter took off his coat.

"I have the phone book right here and found three possible companies, do you want me to go down the list and start calling?" Casey asked.

"Please and I'll fix everyone breakfast." He walked past her and kissed her cheek.

I followed T.J. into the kitchen; Captain was already waiting for breakfast.

Captain has sure gotten his confidence hasn't he T.J.?

You bet, it's great. It's good we get along with each other too. T.J. answered.

Why not get along? It's such a drag to be jealous of each other. Casey and I have seen dogs fight in a family and it just isn't my motto. I told him.

I've always been an only dog, so this is fun having others to go on adventures with. T.J. barked.

"Guys, you have a lot to say this morning, want to share it with me?" Peter laughed as he placed our dishes down for us to eat.

I just wagged my tail and gobbled my food.

Casey walked into the room, "The glass company will be here shortly and repair the damage. Do you need to let your friend know?"

"He's in Spain right now; I'll tell him when he gets back. Let's clean up the glass in the room after we eat and get this day going." Peter handed Casey some coffee.

"Deal." Casey said.

"I need to contact the race commission and let them know what has happened, too. They won't be too happy about this." Casey added.

"After we get back to the villa, why don't you do that Casey?"

"Ok," she answered.

The police came and took photos of the footprints, the glass people came after they left and repaired the window. Then we piled in the Jeep and Peter drove us to his villa to meet Andre, and for Casey to make her phone call.

On the way up to our villa I looked at the neighbors, there were two on the left and three on the right. The closest to Peter's house on the right was a little Bavarian Villa; a retired school teacher lived there with her cat. She was a sweet little old lady; she liked us and brought treats over all of the time. The house next to her house was empty, a vacation rental. The one next to that one on the bottom of the hill had a young man that was a chef at the Hotel Eden, St. Moritz renting the place. He worked a lot and probably didn't have anything to do with skiers. The two houses on the left of the road were a mystery to me. Peter and Casey needed to check them out though. It had to be someone close by that was trying to kill us. Someone had tabs on our actions and what we were doing. Now the place we stayed last night wasn't safe, so Peter decided that staying at his place was best. He knew the inns and outs of most everyone around his place.

Andre met us right after we arrived. Introductions were made all around, and then Casey asked him a question.

"Andre, can you fill us in on anything with this horse race?"

"I would be delighted to my dear." Andre took a seat.

He was a big guy, white hair, dressed in snow boots, a big black parka, ski pants and he had a big moustache.

"Let me get you some tea," Casey said, "don't start until I get back."

She hurried back and handed the cup to Andre.

"Thank you dear, let's see, oh yes, the race. This is a race that people from all over the world will attend; fine thoroughbreds from all over Europe and international jockeys come to take part in the races at White Turf St. Moritz. The race is on the frozen Lake of St. Moritz, it's an amazing scene with the magnificent mountains in the background. Engadine Valley is amazing and beautiful. There is no other race like this one in the world! Men on skis are pulled along a track by unsaddled Thoroughbreds at speeds of up to 50 km/h. The race is over a period of three Sundays. There are other races as well, but this one is the unique one. There will be a tent city covering 130,000 square miles of the iced over Lake of St. Moritz.

This is not only a race! But a social and sporting event that with people from all over coming here.

There will be two grandstands that will hold 2,000 people; therefore, many food vendors will make money.

The cash prizes are very generous; the prize money totals up to half a million Swiss francs. This is called the "European Cup on Snow." It's the most highly prized race in Switzerland! It has been going on for almost 100 years!" Andre proudly finished speaking and took a sip of his tea.

"That's amazing, someone wants that money bad enough to sabotage the other competitors!" Casey was amazed.

So was I.

"Excuse me a minute while I make a phone call." Casey got up and left the room, when she got back she said, "They want me to be in touch, I didn't tell them the details of what happened to us today though."

"I agree." Peter looked worried.

"We need to go back to the barns and mingle; we need to watch anything suspicious that is going on. It is a good idea to have T.J. and Jackie Lee there to keep an eye on people; you should have Captain on a leash and keep him with you for protection." Andre stood up, "Shall we depart? I have my truck outside; we can go in that unless you want to follow me in your Jeep?"

"We'll follow you in case Casey needs to bring the dogs back before we're done, Andre." Peter said.

"Just follow me then." Andre walked out and we followed.

He took us to the makeshift stables; it was fascinating walking through the busy barns. Casey and

Peter met some interesting people. T.J. and I wandered around and kept our eyes on anyone suspicious.

I was walking by a paddock with T.J.; we were three barns back from Casey when we heard something! I walked a little faster, T.J. was right behind me. The door was open and someone was in a stall, he was bent over and he had sprinkled something in the water dish!

I barked and jumped on him, knocking him over!

The guy screamed!

T.J. get Peter, Casey or Andre, hurry, I'll hold him.

Right away Jackie Lee!

T.J. took off, the trainer came in.

"Get this dog off me!!!" Screamed the guy.

The trainer took his stick and started swinging it at me. I growled and showed my teeth.

He backed off and called for help.

"What's going on here?" Andre appeared with T.J.

"Get that dog off the man!" Shouted the trainer glaring at Andre.

"Put your stick down! Jackie Lee is a good dog and he sensed something wrong!" Andre rushed passed the trainer. The trainer lowered his stick and backed out of the stall.

"Good job Jackie Lee." Andre came over and put cuffs on the guy, I let go of him.

"This dog was just doing his job," Andre told the trainer. "I suggest you have that water tested now! I think Jackie Lee found this guy doing something in here that shouldn't have been done."

"What do you mean?" The caretaker was getting red in the face. "If this man has done anything to hurt my horse I'll press charges!"

He turned, "Johnny, get a fresh bucket of water in here now!"

The young boy ran off to do as he was told.

"Can you take that bucket out? I need to take a sample of the water to the station and have it tested. I'm Andre, a policeman."

"Yes, sorry, I'm Francois, one of the caretakers of Carson City Spirit, she has a good chance to win this event and if anything were to happen to her, I don't know what I'd do? The owners will be very upset about this. I don't know who this man is."

"I'm taking him down to the station to find out. You must have Carson City Spirit guarded by someone you strongly trust, whoever is doing this is going to try again to harm her. Thanks for the water." Johnny sat down the container of water for Andre to take with him.

"I will contact the owners and we will move her, putting a guard on her." Francois was furious.

Peter and Casey showed up, Peter took the crook from Andre.

"Jackie Lee, good boy!" Casey hugged me.

"Casey, why don't you follow us to the station, I'll ride with Andre and we'll talk after that." Peter patted my head.

"Good job Jackie Lee!"

I gave him high five.

It was a good feeling to get him, Peter.

"I'm sure I understood that bark Jackie Lee," Peter laughed.

"Come on Jackie Lee, T.J. and Captain, let's go, I'll see you down at the station." Casey said looking back at Peter.

We got to the station and the suspect was put into a cell. Andre filled out the paperwork and then came back out to meet Peter and Casey. We made it to the station before them and I was inside with Casey; T.J. and Captain were in the Jeep outside waiting for us.

"This is looking more and more like an inside job, we'll have the test's back this afternoon from the lab. Casey, whoever is plotting this will not stop at killing anyone! I know you were hired by the committee of this event to keep it safe, but I'm imploring you to let them think you are, but don't report everything we find to them. There is a leak on the inside; it isn't an outsider doing this. Can you do this?" Andre asked Casey.

"Yes, I have to agree with you. We are in grave danger and I believe that now Carson City Spirit is the horse they are going to do away with unless we stop them!" Casey looked at me.

"I'm worried about the danger to our dogs though." Casey added.

"That is why I'm telling you not to go anywhere or be left alone. You must insist Jackie Lee does not take off to solve this crime on his own." Andre told her.

Casey looked at me and shook her head, "Do you hear what he just said, Jackie Lee?"

Woof! *I hear you but it won't happen if any of us are in danger.* I barked at her.

"Well, Jackie Lee had a lot to say." Peter laughed.

"I don't think he agreed." Casey told him.

"Regardless, we are in agreement? Yes?" Andre asked.

"Yes," Casey and Steve both said together.

We said our goodbyes, decided to meet again after lunch.

I jumped into the Jeep next to T.J. and told both of the dogs what had happened. T.J. gave me a high five; we were going to solve this together!

Peter pulled up in front of St. Moritz Grill, "I'll go in and order food to go Casey, then we can go back home and eat. That way the dogs won't get cold waiting for us."

"Great idea, hold on. Casey looked the menu up on her I-Phone. Hmmm, how about an order of Red Crab Cake and an order of the Wood-Grilled Shrimp Cocktail for us to share and then look here," she showed him the menu, "do you want to share an entrée?"

Peter looked, "Yes, let's get the crab cake and shrimp dishes, then I would like the Turkey Panini or the Cuban Panini, which one?" Peter asked Casey.

"The Cuban Panini." She smiled at him, "I know how you love those."

"Ok, I'll be right back." Peter left the Jeep running so we would be warm and went inside. He came back out in twenty minutes with yummy smelling food.

I licked my lips. Casey took the sack from Peter and looked at me. I'll fix you guys a snack back at the villa, Jackie Lee." Casey laughed and turned back around.

They let us out at the villa and I jumped out relieving myself, and then ran into the house to join the others.

After lunch, Peter told us that we had better stay home, he was going to take Casey back to the stables and we could watch the house. I really knew that he didn't trust us not to get into some trouble.

So, Casey told us to be good and left with Peter. As soon as the door was shut, I turned to the others. We need to find out who tried to kill Casey and me, who's in?

I'm in! T.J. barked. We both looked at Captain.

Maybe I should stay here? Captain barked.

Probably a good idea, you can protect the place, we'll be back before Casey and Peter. Follow me T.J. I trotted off toward the garage, I slipped through the kitchen door and T.J. followed. The garage had a button to open the door and I hit it with my paw. Up went the garage door. I couldn't close it from the outside, oh well, Captain was in the house to protect it. T.J. and I took off across the yards, a shortcut to the stables.

Finally, at the stables we entered the aisle that Carson City Spirit's stall was in yesterday. It was empty.

I heard someone talking and coming our way. Hurry T.J. in here!

We flew behind the storage door across from Carson City Spirit's stall.

We listened.

"That pesky German Shepherd has to be caught and gotten rid of." One man was saying.

My eyes grew huge and I looked at T.J. *He's talking about me!*

I know, listen. T.J. said.

We listened more intently.

"We could have drugged and horse napped Carson City Spirit except for that dog! They have her under guard night and day now; I don't know how we can get her alone?" The same man said.

"We could drug the guard, or kill him." Another man said, who had a deep husky voice with a German accent.

"It would be too suspicious after trying to kill that dog and woman yesterday. I don't want to be caught." The first man said.

They weren't saying their names and I couldn't get a glimpse of them without revealing our identity.

"If we don't let him know who drugged him, we don't have to kill him. I'm not doing this for that reason. We need the horse until after the race and we'll hold her for ransom. That way Native Bid will win, we'll put all our money on him and then get a bonus from the owner for training him so well!" The first man said.

"Ok, so here's the plan........

I looked at T.J. We didn't hear the plan but we found out it's the trainer for Native Bid! Let's go find Casey; they plan on horse napping Carson City Spirit!

146

Jackie Lee, how do we convince Casey and Peter to understand what we just heard?

We can't so maybe we had just better try and find out where Carson City Spirit is being held to help her!

Great idea! T.J. barked.

I stuck my head out the door and looked, the coast was clear. We got out of the aisle and walked like we were supposed to be there until we came to the last row of stalls in Aisle Ten. I stopped in my tracks and T.J. almost ran into me. I looked both ways; our only hiding place was under the horse trailer. I dashed under it and T.J. followed.

That was close! T.J. barked.

Too close, there's Casey and Peter talking to the owner of Carson City Spirit.

"I have a guard on her around the clock, when she goes out to practice she's got a crowd around her, so she's as safe as I can keep her. She has a good chance at winning the race and I want her to be safe." Baron Aldman, the owner of Carson City Spirit told Casey and Peter. "I want to thank you for saving her the other day and I'm sorry you were almost killed the other day."

"You're most certainly welcome, and thank you, that was a horrifying experience! Peter and T.J. saved us. I'm forever thankful." Casey added looking at Peter.

"It's my concern they will kill whomever gets in their way and if they get to Carson City Spirit, it's all over. Do you trust your trainer?" Peter asked Baron Aldman.

"I do, his name is Marchion Hemburg, his father was my trainer before him. I have known him since he was a young boy, he is like family. Marchion grew up around my horses and he has always been honest and dependable. He wants for nothing, because I treat him very well. Do you think he is in danger as well?" Baron Aldman asked.

"I think we are all in danger, even you. I want a guard on you as well as Marchion." Peter told him.

Baron turned around and said, "Follow me, I'll make a call and hire some guards right now."

With that they disappeared from our view and hearing range.

Let's get back home before they do T.J. We have to figure out a way to tell Casey and Peter what we know.

I have an idea Jackie Lee, if we go right now up to them and let them know we are here then they will think that maybe we know something. If they just see us at home, they will think we have been home and know nothing new.

You're right T.J.! Let's go find them now!

We crawled out from under cover of the horse trailer and ran into the aisle looking for Casey and Peter.

Casey's eyes got big when she saw us. "Jackie Lee! T.J.! How did you get here?"

Woof woof! I said wagging my tail.

Peter turned to Baron and said, "These are your real detectives, let us introduce them."

Casey said, "This is Jackie Lee." I gave him a high five. Baron laughed.

Then Peter said, "Let me introduce you to T.J." T.J. offered his paw.

"Well, let me say, this is a delight to meet both of you. How much did you hear and where have you been? I bet you know something to help us."

Baron was intuitive, I must say. If only we could tell him what we know.

Baron made his call to hire guards then told us he was going to stay in his office until his hired guard appeared. He thanked us, Peter and Casey exchanged numbers, T.J. and I got a ride home with Peter and Casey.

As we approached Peter's place, he said, "Look at that Casey, they opened the garage door to get out."

"I think we had better start taking them with us," Casey laughed. "I bet poor Captain is frightened.

We got out the Jeep and piled into the house. Captain was whining and very happy to see all of us.

That night I had a dream.......

I was on a train, it was going fast, I had been put on it but all I could see was Casey Lane running after me as the train went faster and faster; she disappeared and all my hope was gone.

Casey shook me awake. "Jackie Lee you were howling; it was just a bad dream boy. I'm here."

I licked her and fell back asleep into her arms. It wasn't long after that we heard the phone ring. I heard Peter answer it and then he came running into our room.

"Casey!" she sat up in bed.

"What is it Peter? Casey asked worriedly as she slipped out of bed into her slippers, and then grabbed her robe.

"That was Baron, Carson City Spirit's guard was just found dead and she is gone!"

ABOUT THE AUTHOR

MICHELE WRITES UNDER the pen name of JMM Adams. She lives in the North West with her beloved German Shepherds, Horse and parrot. A new book will be out next year, it's a mystery with Casey Lane and Jackie Lee. Casey Lane finds out some dark secrets about her grandfather and in seeking the truth, she puts herself and Jackie Lee in jeopardy.

Be sure to catch all of the blogs and updates on new material on Facebook under Author JMMAdams, twitter and www.jmmadams.com